SCARECROW

SCARE

CROW

by Vladimir Zheleznikov

translated from the Russian
by Antonina W. Bouis

J. B. LIPPINCOTT New York

Scarecrow
Copyright © 1983 by Detskaya Literatura
English translation copyright © 1990 by Harper & Row, Publishers, Inc.
First published in the U.S.S.R. by Molodaya Gvardia, 103030, Moscow, K-30
Sushachevokaya, 21, under the title *Chuchelo.*
Printed in the United States of America. For information
address J. B. Lippincott Junior Books, 10 East 53rd Street, New York, NY 10022.
Typography by Joyce Hopkins
1 2 3 4 5 6 7 8 9 10
First American Edition, 1990

Library of Congress Cataloging-in-Publication Data
Zheleznikov, V. (Vladimir)
 [Chuchelo. English]
 Scarecrow / by Vladimir Zheleznikov ; translated from the Russian
by Antonina W. Bouis.
   p.   cm.
 Translation of: Chuchelo.
 Summary: Twelve-year-old Lena comes to live with her eccentric
grandfather in a small Russian town and finds herself mocked and
persecuted by a gang of her classmates at her new school.
 ISBN 0-397-32316-6.—ISBN 0-397-32317-4 (lib. bdg.)
 [1. Prejudices—Fiction. 2. Gangs—Fiction. 3. Soviet Union—
Fiction.] I. Title.
PZ7.Z455Sc   1990   90-6698
[Fic]—dc20   CIP
                                                        AC

Dear Friends!

The mystery of the soul has always been of great interest to me. In my book *Scarecrow* I write about teenagers trying to discover that mystery. For me it is the movement of Russian soul and Russian character, its transformation under the influence of circumstances, and its features that do not change.

Now let me say a few words about myself, so that you will have an idea about the author of this book who lives many thousand kilometers away from your country. I was born in the town of Vitebsk, a small town known to the entire world because it is the birthplace of the great painter Marc Chagall. For many years now, I have been living in Moscow. My apartment is just a stone's throw from the Kremlin. I am married and I am proud of my wife, not only because I love her, but also because we have different views on many problems, and she helps me to widen my perception of the world around me. I have a daughter who is a pianist and a granddaughter who is a ballet dancer. My hobby, which is the cinema, takes up most of my free time. I am an artistic director of the Globus movie studio that makes films for teenagers.

Although I write only for children and teenagers, I seldom think of my own childhood—it is like a broken vessel, the pieces of which are scattered before my mental image. I take a much keener interest in today's teenagers. I think of myself as being fortunate to have a chance to reexperience that period of life—an age filled with hopes and optimism, hovering between imagination and reality—a blessed state of mind. Adults like to think that they exercise a strong influence over children, but in reality it is the children who have a stronger influence on the adult world. And this may be the most important aspect of life, because our future depends upon it.

Many of my books have been published in other countries — Japan, Yugoslavia, Czechoslovakia, Denmark, Poland, Germany, Bulgaria.

Scarecrow is my first book to be translated into English. Two times I have been awarded the State Prize of the Soviet Union. Twice I have been awarded prizes abroad — in Italy and in Poland. The Polish prize has a special meaning for me because it is named for the well-known educator and martyr, Janusz Korczak, a brave man who died in a concentration camp together with his pupils, who were executed for being Jewish.

I hope you will like my story, if only because it will give you an idea about another country and about different kinds of people. I'll be happy if after reading this book you will feel like dropping me a line.

My address: Vladimir Zheleznikov, Kotelnicheskaya naberezhnaya, 1/15. Bldg. B, Apt. 83, Moscow, USSR.

I wish you happiness!

Sincerely yours,
V. Zheleznikov

Prologue

"Scare-crow! . . . Scarc-crow!" echoed painfully in Lena's ears.

She was running down the narrow, hilly streets, seeing nothing in her path. Past the one-story houses with lace curtains and tall TV antennas. Past long fences and gates, with cats in the cornices and dogs at the doors.

"Grandfather!" she sobbed as she ran. "Let's go away! Away! Let them attack each other! Wolves! . . . Foxes! . . . Jackals! . . . Please, Grandfather!"

"She's nuts!" shouted the passersby as she bumped into them.

"Who is she?"

"That's old man Bessoltsev's granddaughter."

They shook their heads — sadly, sympathetically, disapprovingly.

For a number of years Lena's grandfather, Nikolai Nikolayevich Bessoltsev, had been living in the house of his ancestors in an old Russian town on the Oka River. The town was over eight hundred years old, rich in history and tradition. The black Bessoltsev house, with ornamented balconies on the second floor and a breezy wraparound porch on the first, did not resemble its neighbors but stood out like a raven among a flock of colorful birds.

Nikolai Nikolayevich had arrived early one spring, when the earth was damp and cold from recently melted snow. He had not been in the town for over thirty years. As he approached his house, he felt a lump in his throat and his heart began thumping. He stood for a few seconds looking at the shuttered windows and boarded gate, before he crossed the street with a determined tread and tore the boards off the gate. Then he found an ax in the shed and began knocking down the boards from the windows.

Nikolai Nikolayevich remembered the house as big and roomy, smelling of the warmth of the stoves, baked bread, steamed milk, and fresh-washed floors. When he was a child Nikolai Nikolayevich always thought that besides the "real" people — his grandmother and grandfather, father and mother, brothers and sisters, countless visiting aunts and uncles — there also lived with them the people in the paintings hung on the walls of all the rooms.

Men and women in homespun clothes, with kind and stern faces. Women in gold-embroidered dresses with trains, diadems sparkling in their high hairdos. Men in blindingly white, blue, and green top hats with high-standing collars, in boots with gold and silver spurs. A portrait of the famous General Rayevsky, in parade uniform, hung in the best spot.

The feeling that the people in the paintings actually lived in their house never left him, even in the thirty years he was away. Nikolai Nikolayevich's great-grandfather had been an artist, and his father, Dr. Bessoltsev, had spent many years of his life collecting his works. The portraits were an important part of their family heritage.

Nikolai Nikolayevich bypassed the entry, a small corridor with the back stairs to the second floor, and with trepidation opened the door to the big room they formally called the parlor. The walls were bare—all the portraits were gone!

The house smelled damp and neglected. There were cobwebs on the ceiling and in the corners. Fear and horror overwhelmed Nikolai Nikolayevich—the portraits were gone! He tried to take a step, but slipped and barely kept his balance: The floor had a thin layer of ice.

Another room.

Another.

Not a painting anywhere!

Suddenly Nikolai Nikolayevich remembered: Just before she had died, his sister had written that she had taken down all the portraits, wrapped them in burlap, and stacked them in the loft.

Nikolai Nikolayevich hurriedly climbed to the loft and with trembling hands pulled out one painting after another, afraid that they were ruined.

But it was a miracle — the paintings were safe.

Nikolai Nikolayevich lit every stove in the house, opened every window, washed the walls, cleaned the ceilings, and scrubbed the floors, board by board.

Gradually Nikolai Nikolayevich felt the warmth of the family stoves and the familiar smells of his ancestral home. He took the slipcovers off the furniture and, at last, hung up the portraits — each in its proper place.

Nikolai Nikolayevich looked around. More than anything he wanted to sit in his father's old chair, which he had been forbidden to do as a child. Now he slowly sank into the chair, leaned back against its softness, and let his thoughts drift off into the past.

The house came alive, talking, singing, weeping. Many people drifted into the room and made a circle around Nikolai Nikolayevich. He saw his son come in. He had always hoped his son would settle down in the old Bessoltsev home one day instead of going off on some expedition or other.

When he opened his eyes, sunlight was streaming into the house and falling onto the portrait of General Rayevsky. Nikolai Nikolayevich remembered how as a child he used to catch the first rays of the sun on that painting, and laughed sorrowfully and happily, thinking that his life had passed. Then he went out onto the porch and saw the sunlight on the east balcony, beginning yet another circle around the house.

Years passed. People got used to seeing Nikolai Nikolayevich running headlong down the narrow streets, with his cap low on his forehead and his worn coat mended with big, neat patches on the elbows, sometimes carrying packages wrapped in cloth—his face glowing with happiness. Some knew he was searching out paintings, spending almost all his money on them. The rest he spent for firewood, to keep the house dry so the family portraits wouldn't get damp.

Then one day Nikolai Nikolayevich appeared in town not alone but accompanied by a girl. He stopped everyone on the street and repeated

the same phrase over and over: "This is Lena
. . . my granddaughter. . . . . She's come to live
with me while her father is away." As if she
were some world-famous celebrity.

Lena grew very embarrassed every time he
said it. She was an awkward thirteen-year-old,
a calf on long legs, with long, clumsy arms.
Her shoulder blades stuck out like wings. Her
mobile face had a large mouth that was almost
always fixed in a friendly smile. Her hair was
braided into two taut plaits.

Nikolai Nikolayevich's life did not change
much after Lena's arrival except that now he
would occasionally go to the market for meat,
which he had never done before. In the fall
Lena started to go to the local school, and that's
when the whole story began.

1

It was in early November. Lena was running down the crooked streets oblivious to everything around her. She did not hear people's voices, did not see where the streets were taking her. Lena felt alone and unwanted, and she wanted to leave town immediately.

Nikolai Nikolayevich was busy dusting the family portraits with a fine bristle brush. He didn't notice when Lena burst into the room, her lips in a tight line, her eyes filled with despair.

Lena shook the textbooks and notebooks out of her bag and began shoving whatever things of hers were handy into the bag.

"Easy! Easy!" Nikolai Nikolayevich shook his head sadly. "Why are you stomping around like an elephant, raising dust from the floorboards? Why don't you look around! See how much

1

beauty surrounds you. These paintings are over a hundred years old, and they grow more beautiful with every year. . . ."

"Give me some money, I'm leaving," said Lena, fastening her bag.

"Are you going far?" Nikolai Nikolayevich was brushing General Rayevsky's medals.

"Today is Dimka Somov's birthday party," Lena said.

"And you're not invited, so you're leaving? You get too excited. Too sensitive. . . . Follow General Rayevsky's example—"

"Please, Grandfather, give me money for a boat ticket," Lena interrupted.

"Where are you thinking of going?" Nikolai Nikolayevich looked at Lena for the first time.

"To my father," Lena said.

"To your father!" Here Nikolai Nikolayevich forgot about his paintings and jumped down from his stool. "Don't even think of it!" He shook his finger at her. "What will you think of next! I can't leave this place!"

"I don't need you!" Lena shouted. "I'll go by myself!"

Nikolai Nikolayevich surveyed his portraits and spoke in a very quiet voice. "You have to understand, child, this is all I live for." He reached out toward Lena. "Give me your bag."

Lena jumped away and shouted, "Give me

the money!"

"You're not going anywhere, understand?" said Nikolai Nikolayevich. "Just stop all this nonsense."

"Give me money!" Lena was crazed. "Otherwise I'll—I'll steal something and sell it."

Nikolai Nikolayevich laughed. "We have nothing to sell."

Lena looked around helplessly, then suddenly shouted, "I'll sell one of your paintings!" She grabbed the closest painting from the wall.

"My portraits?" Nikolai Nikolayevich moved swiftly forward and without realizing it slapped Lena's face. He stepped back in horror.

Lena picked up her bag and ran for the door. Nikolai Nikolayevich tried to grab her, but she pulled away and ran out of the house.

"No! Lena, stop!" he shouted. "You're crazy!" Hurrying, his arm missing the sleeve of his coat, he ran out of the house after her.

In the meantime Val was running along the riverbank, dressed up in a clean shirt and tie. He had a dog leash and collar in his hand, and he kept kicking cans left littering the bank by summer tourists. He was trying to hit birds and chickens pecking in the brush, or cats soaking up the last sunshine. If he managed to hit one, his own cleverness made him terribly happy.

Val stopped by an old oak — two boys' heads were sticking out of its trunk. "What are you doing in there, you little punks?" Val barked.

"Nothing," they replied. "We're playing fireman."

"Out of there!" Val slapped his rubber boot with the leash. "Pick up those leaves! Stuff them in the hole! Move it!"

The boys picked up piles of leaves and stuffed them into the tree trunk. When it was full, Val lit a match and threw it in on the leaves. Then with a shout of "Go on, firemen, do your stuff!" he walked away.

Val was hurrying to meet his friends, to go to Dimka Somov's party. He saw Shaggy and Red sitting on the bench near the ferry landing and plopped himself down next to them. "Hey, guys, ready to chow down?" he asked. "When I think of the pies at Somov's, I start drooling."

"I'm bringing honey," Shaggy said.

"My granny didn't give me anything," said Val. "Why bring food where there's going to be plenty, she says."

"You've got a clever granny," Shaggy said.

"She may be clever, but she's not rich," said Val. "Now take Somov. He was born with a silver spoon in his mouth. And he's good-looking, he gets straight A's. I'd really like to re-arrange his face for him. . . ."

"You're just jealous," Shaggy said.

"And you're not?" Val asked.

"What do I have to be jealous about?" Shaggy said. "I can beat up anyone I want."

"So what?" Val spat scornfully. "Strength isn't money. You can't buy butter with it."

Shaggy grabbed Val's neck with one hand and pressed hard.

"Let go!" shouted Val.

"Red, what's most important in a man?" asked Shaggy.

"Strength!" said Red.

"Val doesn't respect that," Shaggy said. "He says the most important thing is money."

"Let go!" Val begged. "I respect strength, I do! Let go! You're choking me!"

Shaggy let go.

Val rubbed his neck. "You have the strength of a tractor. Not like your father. . . ." He was going to add something else, but thought better of it.

"Leave my father out of it," Shaggy said.

"Look who's coming!" said Red. "Shmakova!"

Shmakova was accompanied by Popov, but the others ignored Popov and stared at her. She didn't walk, she floated. Next to her Popov looked awkward and pitiful. Shmakova was dressed all in white; even the ribbon in her hair was all white.

5

"Wow! A vision in white," cried Val.

"You look like a movie star," said Shaggy.

"Somov will flip," Red said.

"I don't care about Somov," said Shmakova, pleased with herself.

"That's what you say," said Shaggy.

"Ha!" said Val.

"Ha-ha!" added Red.

Popov looked at Shmakova, and his round, snub-nosed face took on a sorry expression. "Hey, guys, stop it," he pleaded. "Why don't we just go to Somov's."

"We have to wait for Mironova," said Shaggy.

"The hell with Mironova," Val said. "Who is she anyway?"

"We'll wait for Iron Button," Shaggy said loudly.

"Sure, sure, we'll wait," Val agreed. "Besides, Vasiliev isn't here either."

Then they saw Vasiliev, a skinny kid in glasses.

"You didn't have to wait for me." Vasiliev said. "I'm not going to Somov's."

"Why not?" demanded Shaggy, just as Mironova appeared. As usual, her hair was neatly done and under her jacket she wore her brown school uniform.

"Hi, Mironova," Shaggy said.

"Hi, Iron Button," said Val.

Slowly she made her way past them and stood

in front of Vasiliev. "So, Vasiliev, why aren't you going to Somov's party?" she asked.

"Got errands to do," Vasiliev said, raising his net shopping bag filled with groceries.

"You're lying," said Mironova.

Vasiliev was silent: The thick lenses of his glasses made his eyes look big and round.

"Well, why are you silent?" Mironova persisted.

"I don't feel like going." Vasiliev gave Mironova a challenging look. "I'm sick of Dimka Somov."

"Sick, you say?" Mironova gave Shaggy a meaningful look.

Shaggy moved forward, and the others followed.

"Do you know what people get for lying?" Mironova asked.

"What?" Vasiliev's round eyes stared at her.

"This!" Shaggy swung back and punched Vasiliev.

Vasiliev fell, his glasses flying off. He dropped the shopping bag and the groceries fell out.

Everyone waited to see what would happen next.

Vasiliev got up on all fours and began feeling around for his glasses. No one helped.

"You've turned into vicious beasts!" he shouted.

"Get going!" Shaggy pushed him. "Or I'll give you more!"

Vasiliev shoved the groceries back into the bag. "Savages!" he repeated as he scampered off to the sound of the others laughing.

"Our gang is losing ranks," Red said.

"But we're strong," Mironova pronounced.

"We'll attack Somov's pies united!" shouted Val.

"Stop joking," Mironova said. "This is serious."

Just as they were turning to go, they caught sight of Margarita Ivanovna, their homeroom teacher.

"Let's split before she sees us," Red suggested, "or she'll start lecturing."

"I'm not a jumping bean," Mironova sneered.

"Why don't we hide and scare her?" Val said.

"Now that's an idea," said Shmakova.

They scattered—all except Mironova, who unhurriedly walked behind a tree.

Val crept up behind their teacher and shouted in her ear: "Hello, Margarita Ivanovna!"

Margarita Ivanovna started and spun around.

"Did I scare you?" Val asked innocently. "Hey, guys, I scared Margarita Ivanovna."

"I was lost in thought," Margarita Ivanovna apologized, blushing. "You all look so nice," she said. "And Shmakova looks very grown-up."

8

"Do you like my dress?" Shmakova purred with pleasure.

"I do," Margarita Ivanovna replied. "Who made it for you?"

"You know who!" Popov announced proudly. "My mother!"

"Under my direction," Shmakova added. She whispered angrily to Popov, "Who asked you? Maybe I had it sent from Moscow, from the fashion house. 'My mother, my mother.' "

"Why aren't you dressed up, Mironova?" Margarita Ivanovna asked.

"Me? I can't stand frills." Mironova looked haughtily at her friends. "Excuse us, Margarita Ivanovna, we're late."

"Where are you going?" Margarita Ivanovna was taken aback by Mironova's abruptness.

"Somov's," Red replied. "Birthday party."

"Give him my best," said Margarita Ivanovna. "And tell him I hope he always stays the way he is now. Have a great time. I have to rush off and meet my new husband." Margarita Ivanovna waved and hurried to the wharf.

"She won't make it to . . ." Mironova began, but the end of the sentence froze on her lips—she caught sight of Lena Bessoltseva.

And Lena saw the gang—she stopped as if planted in the ground. And the gang saw Lena and grinned in delight.

9

Mironova's lips stretched into a measured smile. "Here before us is a historical exhibit— Lena Bessoltseva!"

"Right!" shouted Shaggy.

"Bessoltseva, have you learned your lesson?" asked Mironova.

Lena did not reply. She stood without moving.

"She's not answering," Val said in disappointment. "I guess she hasn't learned."

"Maybe she's deaf?" Shmakova whispered. "Why don't you . . . shake her up?"

Val made a fist to hit Lena's thin back.

"That's not necessary," Mironova said.

The others shouted: "Tattletale!"

"We don't need people like you."

"Scarecrow!" Val grabbed Lena's arm and pulled her into the middle of their circle. They leaped around Lena, mocking her.

"Scare-crow! Scare-crow!"

"Big Mouth!"

"Ugly Face!"

Lena struggled to get out as they spun around her.

Just then Nikolai Nikolayevich appeared. "Stop it!" he shouted. "Leave her alone!"

"Old Patches to the rescue!" Red yelled.

But they all scattered. Only Mironova remained, totally unmoved. Her words were filled with scorn for the others. "What's the matter with all of you?"

"Six against one!" Nikolai Nikolayevich's voice was tragic. "You should be ashamed of yourselves!"

"Why should we?" Val asked. "We aren't doing anything illegal."

"Your granddaughter's the one who should be ashamed," Mironova said.

"Lena!" Nikolai Nikolayevich asked in surprise. "Why?"

Lena turned toward her grandfather, and he saw her face: distorted, petrified.

"Ask *her*," Mironova said. "Let's go, gang."

In the quiet, transparent autumn air their shouts echoed after them: "Hail to Iron Button!"

"You didn't let Patches scare you!"

"Victory in strength!"

Lena pressed her face against Nikolai Nikolayevich's chest.

"Don't, child." He patted the soft nape of her neck. "Don't pay any attention to them." His voice trembled. "Learn from me. I'm calm, see? Did you hear them call me 'Patches'? Miserable kids! They know not what they do." Suddenly he asked hesitantly and softly, "Why are they treating you that way?"

Lena pulled away from him and turned her head.

I shouldn't have asked her anything, Nikolai

Nikolayevich thought, *but what could she have done that was so terrible?* "Forgive me, child," he said. "You've decided to leave. I lived alone before . . . and I can do it again." He stopped, because he didn't like what those words meant. "I got used to you, I'll get unused. . . . We lived together but I didn't understand you. That's what hurts." He rummaged in his pockets, took out his worn wallet, and spent a long time digging around in it, hoping that Lena would say she had changed her mind about leaving. He was playing for time, sighing deeply, but Lena was silent.

"Here," he said finally, handing her some money. "Buy two tickets for tomorrow. I'll come with you as far as Moscow."

"I want to leave today!" Lena cried. "Today! Right now!"

"But that's crazy," Nikolai Nikolayevich argued. "Look at the things you've taken. Where is your coat? It's been snowing in Moscow, you'll get strep throat! You're . . ."

"Today, now!" Lena kept sobbing. Nikolai Nikolayevich knew his arguments were nonsense; what mattered was that he didn't want Lena to leave. He stopped, bent over, and said in a plaintive voice, "Let's leave tomorrow!"

Lena took the money from his hand.

"Did you hear? I'll go with you tomorrow!"

12

Lena looked at her grandfather's face hidden under the visor of his hat and saw utter misery. "The patch on your elbow has come loose," she said suddenly.

"Have to sew it back on," Nikolai Nikolayevich said, feeling the patch.

"Why don't you buy yourself a new coat?" she asked.

"I don't have the money."

"That's why they say you're a miser." Lena bit her tongue, but it was too late.

"Miser?" Nikolai Nikolayevich laughed. "That's funny." He examined his coat closely. "Do you think it's indecent to go out in it anymore? You know, I love this coat. There's something reassuring about old things. In the morning when I put the coat on, I remember how your grandmother and I bought it years ago."

They stood there, silent, deep in their own thoughts. Lena was the first to break the silence. "All right, we'll go tomorrow," she said softly.

They returned to the house, where the sound of music and shouts rushed in through the windows. "Party at the Somov's," Nikolai Nikolayevich said. Realizing he had said the wrong thing, he casually closed the windows. But the music and laughter were so loud that it didn't help. Nikolai Nikolayevich sat down at the piano and started to play, but he broke off and silently, with mute reproach, he looked at Lena.

"Don't look at me like that!" she cried. "You can't stay here all alone! Pack up your paintings and we'll leave now, together!"

"That's impossible." Nikolai Nikolayevich looked at the paintings. "They belong here . . . in this town . . . by this river." He smiled guiltily. "For hundreds of years. . . . My life is the continuation of someone else's. Sometimes it seems to me that it wasn't my great-grandfather who painted them, but me. . . . You're the only one I can tell this to. Your father doesn't understand. And when you came here, I foolishly thought that you'd stay here with me forever in the old family home."

Nikolai Nikolayevich walked over to Lena. "Listen. Why don't you go back to school. We'll fight this thing through together."

Like a shot Lena flew to the door.

Nikolai Nikolayevich blocked her way.

"Get away from me!" she screamed. Her lips and face were white as chalk.

Nikolai Nikolayevich moved away from the door and sat down on the couch. Lena hesitated, lowered her head guiltily, and sat down next to him. "Don't be angry with me, Grandfather," she said. "I'm just a loser. I do everything wrong. Please forgive me, Grandfather."

Lena smiled broadly and Nikolai Nikolayevich also smiled. Her face was open and happy, her mouth stretched to her ears, her cheeks grew round. Then her face changed and she looked desperate. "I'll tell you everything, Grandfather. Only don't interrupt, okay? Or I'll get confused and won't be able to tell you."

"All right, child. Calm down and tell me. You'll feel better."

Lena's lips grew tight and her eyes narrowed, and she began her story.

On my first day at school, Margarita Ivanovna, our teacher, called Red into the teachers' room and told him to bring me to the classroom. As Red and I walked down the hallway I kept trying to get him to like me—I kept smiling at him. He just laughed. I have this stupid smile—all the way to my ears. That's why I used to wear my hair over my ears.

When we reached the room Red pushed ahead, shouting, "Hey guys! This new girl . . ." and started laughing. Then he grabbed my hand and dragged me into the room. Maybe I would have died laughing too, if I were him. It's nobody's fault I'm so funny-looking. I wasn't mad at Red for pulling me inside, but I tripped on the doorstep and went sprawling on the floor. All the kids in the room just stared at me. I got up and smiled—I can't help smiling when people stare at me.

Val shouted, "You've heard of Big Foot. She's Big Mouth!"

Vasiliev stuck his fingers in his mouth, stretched out his lips, and shouted, "I can be Big Mouth too!"

"Hey, guys, she's Patches' granddaughter!" Red shouted.

Lena stopped talking and looked at Nikolai Nikolayevich.

"Go on, go on. Don't be embarrassed," he reassured her.

"I hadn't known anything about your nickname, Grandfather," she said.

"Why do you call my grandfather 'Patches'?" I asked.

"I'm called Shaggy," Shaggy said. "Red is called Red. And your grandfather is called Patches. What's wrong with that?"

"Nothing," I agreed. "So you know my grandfather well?" I asked.

"He's famous," Shaggy said.

"Very famous," said Val. "Once I asked your grandfather why he doesn't keep dogs. You know what he said? 'I don't keep dogs so as not to frighten people.'"

I thought that was wonderful.

The other kids thought so too. "We always

remember those words when the apples in his orchard are ripe and we . . . what's the word I want?"

"*Harvest* them?" Red said.

And they all laughed again.

Lena suddenly stopped and looked at Nikolai Nikolayevich. "I'm so stupid," she said. "I realize only now that they were laughing at *me*." She drew herself up, tall and narrow. "I should have defended you, Grandfather!"

"Nonsense," Nikolai Nikolayevich said. "I don't mind them stealing apples. I often watch them scurry about the garden, stuffing apples inside their shirts. I pretend not to see them, while they swipe apples, not knowing what I would do if I caught them."

"You're so kind! That's what I told them, Grandfather — that you were kind!"

Popov said, "My mother sews patches on his coat. She told him, 'You're a retired officer, you have a pension. It doesn't look right to walk around town in patches.' And he said, 'I don't have any money.' "

"You're kidding, Popov!" Red shouted. "What a miser!"

"No way!" Val said. "He gave my granny three hundred rubles for a portrait. He said it was painted by his great-great-great-great . . ."

They tried to fill in the blank.

"Grandmother!"

"Aunt!"

I began laughing too. It was funny that they changed our great-grandfather into a great-grandmother and a great-aunt, wasn't it?

In fact I would never have stopped laughing if it hadn't been for Val. He thought it was hilarious that my grandfather had bought some portrait for all that money. "Gran almost died of joy. She thought she'd get twenty and he gave her three hundred!" he cried.

"Patches and Lena are a perfect pair!" Red said.

"Grandfather and I are a perfect pair!" I shouted it for some reason.

"What a joke!" shouted Shaggy. "You are a riot, Lena Bessoltseva."

"She's no joke," said Red. "She's a scarecrow — skinny and in rags!"

"Grandfather!" Lena grabbed Nikolai Nikolayevich's hand and kissed it. "Please forgive me!"

"What for?"

"For not realizing they were making fun of you."

"It wasn't your fault, child." He smiled kindly. "Go on."

* * *

Well, when Red called me a scarecrow, Dimka Somov gave him a shove in the back. You know, I had liked Dimka right away. He has deep-blue eyes and white-blond hair. And he's all mysterious-looking.

Anyway he pushed Red hard, and hit Popov in the stomach, and a fight started to break out. I wanted to cry out, "Don't fight because of me. So I'm a scarecrow, so what?" I shut my eyes. I always do that when I see fights.

But there was no fight. I heard Dimka say, "Repeat after me, 'I'm a scarecrow, an ordinary red-haired scarecrow.' "

I opened my eyes. Dimka had Red in one arm and was holding him tight. Red made a face and repeated, "I'm an ordinary red-haired scarecrow."

Everyone laughed at him, and he laughed loudest. You've seen Red, Grandfather! He's funny-looking, isn't he? Like a circus clown — he doesn't even need a wig, he's got the red hair.

Then Margarita Ivanovna came in with the roll book in one hand and a plastic bag in the other. She pulled out a box of candy from the bag and put it on her desk.

"From him?" asked Shmakova.

"From him." Margarita Ivanovna glowed with happiness. She was getting married soon, in Moscow. "Help yourselves," she said with a sweep of her arm.

Everyone jumped up and began grabbing those candies and stuffing them into their mouths. I took a candy too. Shmakova stuck one in her mouth and gave the other one to Dimka.

Just then, Mironova appeared in the doorway. They call her Iron Button. She has a small upturned nose and she is the leader; everyone listens to her.

"We're eating candy!" Shmakova said.

"During class?" asked Mironova sharply, and went to her desk.

"Take this and shut up." Shmakova gave her a candy. "Don't criticize us."

"Quiet!" called Margarita Ivanovna. "Mironova is right. Take your seats!"

Everyone went to their desks, except for me. Margarita Ivanovna forgot I was there, and I didn't know where to go, so I stopped near Dimka's desk and stared at him. I have this habit: If I like someone I stare at them. I know it makes people uncomfortable but I can't help it. He looked at me blankly, and then he asked what I wanted.

I burst out with, "Is the seat beside you taken?"

"It is." He smiled and asked, "Why?"

"I wanted to sit with you," I replied.

I think he liked that, because he said, "All right." Then he turned to Shmakova and called,

"Hey, Shmakova, the new girl wants to take your place!"

Shmakova got very angry. She looked in our direction and then started walking toward us slowly. I could see angry fires flickering in her eyes. Shmakova looked me up and down nastily, and turned away. She's really beautiful, Grandfather. And me, I'm just nothing.

"You're wonderful-looking!" said Nikolai Nikolayevich.

"Don't try to console me," said Lena. "Shmakova's beautiful. She was wearing a beautiful new dress. I just have a—a disguised bathrobe."

"A disguised bathrobe?" exclaimed Nikolai Nikolayevich. "I thought your clothes were fine. I should have paid more attention. . . . Lena, you have a radiant face, you have inspired eyes!"

"Please don't praise me," she said. "I'm a bad person."

Lena stopped, and Nikolai Nikolayevich waited patiently for her to continue. The sound of wild music burst into the room again. They were still partying at Dimka Somov's—shouting, singing—while here at the Bessoltsevs' sat two unhappy people, not knowing what to do next.

Nikolai Nikolayevich broke the silence. "Well, what happened with Shmakova?"

*　*　*

With Shmakova? Nothing special—she gave me her seat. She grabbed her book bag and said, "I'm tired of sitting here anyway, the seat is lopsided. And I like a change. So Dimka, ciao!" Then she looked at me, snorted in disgust, and said quietly, "What a scarecrow!" She sat down next to Popov, and he became her slave forever.

Margarita Ivanovna announced that the whole school was going on a trip to Moscow during fall vacation. "So get money for the trip from your parents," she said, smiling.

There was such a burst of joy that it made Margarita Ivanovna laugh and cover her ears. Except for Dimka. He sighed deeply and said, "Using our parents' money again. I'm sick of it."

"What else do you suggest?" asked Margarita Ivanovna. "Would you rather not go to Moscow?"

"No, that's not what he suggests," interrupted Mironova. "He doesn't know what he suggests."

"He knows very well," Shmakova said sweetly. "He's showing off in front of the new girl."

Everyone snickered, but that made me feel good anyway.

Dimka got up, looked at all the kids, and said, "Why can't we *earn* the money for the trip!"

I don't know why, but I jumped up and shouted, "Margarita Ivanovna, Margarita Ivanovna! Can I say something?"

I must have looked like an idiot, but I felt good and I wanted to share the feeling. "My grandfather has told me a lot about your town — it's special, and it's ancient. . . . Once you come here, you don't ever want to leave. It's really wonderful here! And you're all so wonderful! And I support Somov's proposal!" I smiled at Dimka and sat down.

"Well, Somov's idea is good," said Margarita Ivanovna. "I like it very much. I'll postpone my trip to Moscow and help you get jobs. But you have to promise to behave and not to let me down."

Everyone shouted: "We won't, Margarita Ivanovna!"

"We promise!"

"We'll work day and night!"

"From morning to morning!"

And we started working. We worked at the collective farm for the late cucumber and cabbage harvest, and we helped in the kindergarten, and we cleaned up the town square. Not everyone liked that. Val always disappeared when it came time to do the dirty work.

Early one Sunday morning Margarita Ivanovna brought us to an orchard to pick apples. Everyone wore rubber boots except me — my shoes got soaked right away. Dimka noticed and offered me his boots. There he was barefoot in the cold wet grass offering me his wool socks and boots. I hesitated.

"Wow! Somov has class!" cried Shaggy.

"A knight!" Val yelled.

"The Lionhearted!" added Red with a chuckle at his own joke.

"Are we going to stand around courting?" Shmakova said nastily. "I think we came here to work."

Someone giggled again, but Dimka paid no attention, tossed his boots to me, and walked away.

I pulled on his socks—still warm from his feet—and put on the boots.

"You know, Grandfather, it was so much fun! Do you think it was because Dimka gave me his boots?" She gave Nikolai Nikolayevich a sly look.

"No, I think it was because it was so beautiful in the orchard," he replied.

Nikolai Nikolayevich heard her laugh and it made him happy. Lena stared dreamily off into the distance, remembering the orchard festooned with cobwebs, hundreds of lacy hammocks and suspended bridges among the trees, glistening on the grass and bushes. She remembered how she had secretly watched Dimka as he climbed the trees from one end of the orchard to the other in the red rays of the sun. She remembered how they had worked until dinner, then lit a bonfire and baked apples, and how Red had pulled baked apples out of the fire with his bare hands for the girls.

"And then, Grandfather, a strange thing happened. Remember when we worked at the children's toy factory making papier-mâché animal masks, and I had made a rabbit's face?"

Nikolai Nikolayevich nodded.

"Well, everyone brought their masks that night. I put my rabbit face on first."

Dimka had just come back from picking up our pay and everyone ran over to him, excited.

"Red! Bring the piggy bank!" Dimka shouted.

We had gotten this big green cat with a slot in its head. Red put it down in front of Dimka. Dimka began feeling in his pocket, making a real show of it, then pulled out his hand with a bill in it and threw it into the bank.

"Ten!" shouted Shaggy.

"Five more!" Dimka pulled out another bill, then another.

Lena demonstrated how Dimka had waved the money. She couldn't sit still, she jumped up, her face quivering with delight.

* * *

Red wanted to throw some money into the bank too. Dimka gave him a ruble, and Red threw it in.

Then everyone else wanted to do it too. Dimka handed me a ruble and said, "You too, rabbit."

I was so excited that when I grabbed it, it tore in half.

"Dope!" Val yelled. "That's real money!"

I got scared and didn't know what to do. But Dimka came to my rescue. "Don't worry, rabbit," he said. "We'll glue it together later." He handed me the piggy bank. "As the bravest rabbit in the world, you get to protect this marvelous trunk full of jewels."

I grabbed the piggy bank and yelled, "I'm a brave rabbit! I'm the bravest rabbit in the world!"

Red put on his tiger mask and growled at me.

"I'm not afraid! I'm not afraid!" I shouted, and pushed Red away.

Shmakova put on her fox mask and sang in a high voice, "Little gray rabbit, we're going to trick you. We'll get the treasure away from you!" And she pinched me.

I wasn't expecting that. "That hurts!" I shouted.

"If it doesn't hurt, why pinch?" She laughed.

Everyone had their masks on. I was surrounded by wolves, bears, crocodiles — they jumped and roared, attacking me and trying to get to the bank. A bear, I think it was Popov, shouted Shmakova's words — "Little gray rabbit, we're going to trick you. We'll get the treasure away from you!"

Val the wolf yanked one of my braids hard. I got frightened, as if I were surrounded by real beasts and not people.

"Don't! Stop it!" I wanted to take off my mask, but I couldn't because they were pushing me.

"Gotcha, rabbit!" Shmakova sang.

"We're going to skin you, rabbit!" Shaggy roared. They started spinning me.

"Dimka!" I shouted, and fell to the ground, all dizzy.

Dimka helped me up and I told him I had gotten scared.

"Of what?"

"The animals," I said.

"Big deal, you can't even take a joke," Val sneered.

"Little gray rabbit . . . we're going to skin you," Shmakova sang. "You're so high-strung!"

"It's all nonsense!" said Mironova. "She's just putting on an act. Let's go, gang!"

And the whole group followed Iron Button, as if on command. I was ashamed of acting so silly, so I bought everyone ice cream.

Since that day, whenever I look at Shmakova I see a fox, a red fox. And I see a tiger in Red, and Val reminds me of a wolf. But not Dimka, he was kind. "Don't worry," he said. "Anyone can get scared."

Yes, Dimka can be kind. One time, when we were walking home, we saw Val dragging a dog on a leash, a small bowlegged one with big shaggy ears. When Val noticed us, he ducked around a corner. Dimka ran after him, and I followed Dimka. Val had his back against the wall and was staring at us strangely.

"What a nice dog you have." I patted it. "But why is it trembling? Is it sick?"

Val didn't have a chance to answer, because Dimka grabbed him and let the dog loose. "My leash!" shouted Val, trying to get away from Dimka. "Pete! Help!"

I didn't understand why Dimka was so angry or why Val was so worried about the leash and not the dog, or why he was calling for somebody named Pete.

As it turned out, Pete was Val's big brother, and he materialized out of nowhere. "He let my dog loose!" Val whined.

Pete grabbed Dimka and said politely, "Forgive me, pal, but I have to teach you a lesson." He punched Dimka so hard, he flew past me and landed on the ground.

"Learned your lesson?" jeered Val.

"Good-bye, children," said Pete, and they left without looking back.

I was trembling all over. I went over to Dimka. "Are you all right?" I asked.

He rubbed his cheek. "That's the third dog I've saved from that bastard. He sells them for a ruble to the tannery."

"What a creep! Ever since he attacked me in that wolf mask, I see him as a wolf," I told Dimka.

"Well, that's overdoing it a little," he said.

"No, it isn't, he's a wolf, a real wolf," I cried. "All he cares about is money!"

"Pete's worse than Val," Dimka said. "He stuns fish in the river."

"That's disgusting," I said, feeling sick to my stomach. "How can anyone turn in living things to be skinned alive? He's a real wolf. But you, Dimka—you're a hero!"

He got embarrassed. "Cut it out!"

"No, you're a real hero."

I was so happy that I—well, I kissed him on the cheek. He was going to be my best and most trusted and dependable friend.

He was surprised. "What was that for?"

"That's how women used to thank knights," I said. "And you, Dimka, are my knight. You

30

saved that dog from Val and you saved me from him. That dog is happily telling all the dogs in town what a brave knight you are!"

Just then I heard laughter and whistling. I spun around—there were Pete and Val. They had that same poor dog on the leash. They were laughing because they had caught that dog again. They're wolves, not people!

"You're disgusting!" I shouted.

"The maiden is offended," Pete said, making a sad face.

"How about you, knight, are you offended?" Val asked, giving Dimka a shove. He was really brave when his brother was around.

Dimka attacked Val! But Pete grabbed him and picked him up off the ground, and Dimka hung in the air, his legs kicking—you know, Pete is big, about two heads taller than Dimka—and Pete said in a hissing, sweet voice, "Let's have another kiss, pal." He spread his big hand over Dimka's face and turned his head as if he wanted to unscrew it. Dimka was choking—his mouth and nose were covered. "Do me a favor, pal, don't tell anyone our little secret about the dog. Okay?"

"Okay," mumbled Dimka through Pete's fingers, wiggling out of his iron grip.

They went off, dragging that poor dog. I felt so sorry for it. Dimka looked at me, then shook his fist at the brothers and said, very quietly, "Just you wait till you show up at school, Val. Murderers. Skinners."

I cupped my hands around my mouth and shouted so they could hear: "Murderers!"

Pete stopped and looked back in our direction. Dimka grabbed me by the hand and we ran. "Do you think he heard me?"

"Sure he did. You have to be careful around him. Think how much bigger he is—don't go looking for trouble."

It was the last day before the school break and the trip to Moscow. The class rushed into the physics lab with Dimka leading the way, waving the piggy bank. On the board was a note from Margarita Ivanovna, saying that instead of physics there would be a literature class.

"Freedom!" shouted Shaggy. "The physics teacher is sick!"

"Let's all go to the movies!" shouted Red.

Dimka told everyone to stop shouting and read the blackboard.

Shaggy and Red began reading by syllables. When they got to the end of the note, they bleated Margarita Ivanovna's initials like sheep: "Ehehehehem . . . lyiyiyiyi." Others started bleating too.

"Now stop this!" said Dimka. "Let's behave like adults for a change."

"Dimka is so grown-up," said Shmakova. "He

wants to be in charge."

"Hey, guys," cried Popov, trying to impress Shmakova, "Somov wants to be boss!"

Shaggy stepped up to Dimka. "We're tired of you and your piggy bank, Somov," he said. "You're a spoilsport."

"Are you ever!" yelled Red.

Dimka was taken aback. It had been his idea to earn the money for the trip to Moscow, and now they were ganging up on him. Val leaned his shoulder against the door and said casually, "A knight in shining armor!"

Dimka lashed out. "Gang, do you know what Val does in his free—?"

Just then a head reared up behind Val. It was Pete.

"Val, you forgot your book bag," he said. Then he strolled over to Dimka and patted his cheek. "Hello, pal." He sighed. "It's not nice to eavesdrop, but I overheard your conversation and I understand your problem. . . . Seems that the majority wants to participate in cultural amusement, that is, to go to the local movie theater. I think the majority wins, that's the democratic way. So your problem is solved."

He turned to the board and, humming a little tune, erased Margarita Ivanovna's note. "Now you're free as the wind! Be happy, kids! And you, pal"—he turned to Dimka again—"don't pick on my kid brother." He wagged his finger at Dimka, smiled, and left.

In the complete silence that followed Red said uneasily, "Maybe some stranger did come in and erase the note."

"Now you're talking," said Val.

"You mean we didn't read the note?" Shmakova laughed.

"We didn't read it and we don't know anything about it," Popov said.

"Popov's smart," said Shmakova. "Under my tutelage . . ."

"We'll be letting Margarita Ivanovna down!" Dimka tried to stop them.

"Shut up, creep!" Val shouted. "Let's go, gang!"

Everyone headed for the door.

"I don't have any money!" Vasiliev called out.

This is when it really started. Dimka forgot that he had just been trying to keep everyone from going to the movies; he ran into the middle of the classroom and yelled, "Vasiliev! I'll lend you money!" Dimka's voice rang out loudly. "I've got it! Here's our story: We went to visit our sick physics teacher."

"That's using your noodle, Somov!" Red roared his approval.

I laughed with pride at Dimka's quick comeback. He was already giving orders, and he was the first at the door. I followed, even pushed someone aside to keep up with Dimka.

And then Mironova's harsh voice hit us from behind. "I'm not going!"

For a moment Dimka was silent. Then he yelled, "She's against the majority!"

Mironova's eyes flashed in anger.

"What if we beat you up?" Val asked.

"Just try it," Mironova replied, and sat down at her desk.

Everyone was quiet — no one would dare to lift a hand against Iron Button. Dimka suddenly laughed, and I did too, even though I didn't know why I was laughing. Others joined in too, watching Dimka. He must have a reason for laughing.

"Why are we strong, Shaggy?" Dimka asked.

"Strength is in numbers," Shaggy replied. He picked up Iron Button and carried her out of the lab as everyone cheered and laughed. . . .

Lena looked at Nikolai Nikolayevich. Her darting, nervous glance asked for support, understanding. *I'm so stupid,* thought Nikolai Nikolayevich, *so useless.*

Lena smiled weakly and continued.

We had crossed the school yard when Dimka realized he had forgotten the piggy bank. "You

36

shouldn't leave money around," said Val. "It'll go bye-bye."

"I'll get it!" I shouted. In my excitement I tripped over my own feet and landed on the concrete, skinning my knee.

"Clumsy!" said Dimka, and ran back to the school himself.

"Your knight wasn't pleased," taunted Val.

"It doesn't hurt!" I said to Val, but I was ready to weep with pain and embarrassment.

"Why don't you go to the nurse?" Iron Button suggested.

Limping, I headed back to the school. I heard someone laugh behind me, so I laughed too and limped harder to make them all laugh.

As I was passing the physics lab I heard Margarita Ivanovna and Dimka talking. I froze. She had caught him!

"Where are the others?" Margarita Ivanovna wanted to know.

"Gone," said Dimka calmly. "The physics teacher is sick."

"But I left you a note on the board saying there would be a literature class instead."

"Really? We didn't see any note. Someone must have erased it."

"Not 'someone,' but one of you kids," Margarita Ivanovna replied angrily. "I don't like being lied to."

Dimka said he didn't either.

"Then tell me, where did everyone 'split'? That's the expression you use, I believe?"

Dimka said nothing. But Margarita Ivanovna kept after him. She said we were pathetic and petty. That we didn't appreciate fair and good treatment. And right before the trip . . . it really hurt! A knife in the back! Her voice trembled.

Then her voice grew harder. I don't know what prompted her, but she called him a coward.

"Me? A coward?" Dimka raised his voice. "Me?" he shouted.

Suddenly Lena burst into tears.

"Grandfather!" she whispered. "Dimka told her *everything.*"

Nikolai Nikolayevich felt totally helpless and confused. "Then why are they persecuting you?" he asked.

Lena gulped air. The words flew from her lips, louder and faster.

I watched Margarita Ivanovna run out of the room, her heels clicking down the empty corridor, like shots: *rat-a-tat.* Then Dimka rushed past me, waving the piggy bank. Everything was all confused in my mind. I wrapped my hankie around my knee and ran after him.

I caught up with Dimka on the street. He didn't know I had been there and heard everything. When we joined the others, I thought Dimka would tell them what had happened, but he didn't. He didn't tell! I don't know why, maybe he didn't want to spoil their fun? We all went to the movies. All except Shmakova and Popov.

I couldn't concentrate on the movie, I kept thinking about Dimka and Margarita Ivanovna. I hoped he would tell about Margarita Ivanovna after the movie. I was so nervous I was shuddering. Iron Button noticed and asked me what was wrong. I said I didn't know, but I thought, *Maybe Dimka wants to talk to me first. I am his best friend, after all.* But he didn't.

After the movie everyone went home and Dimka and I were left alone. I kept waiting and thinking: *Now he'll tell me.* But he didn't say anything, and I didn't ask.

Afterward, I realized how stupid I had been. Just think, Grandfather, if I had asked, if I had told him I knew everything, it would all have been different.

4.

The next morning everyone came all dressed up for the trip. Except for Mironova—she was wearing her school uniform, as usual. The aisles between the desks were filled with luggage. Margarita Ivanovna arrived in a new pink dress with a white flower print—she would be getting married in Moscow, remember. But she didn't look happy. She had a sheet of paper in her hand, a ruling from the principal. You know what it said, Grandfather? "For cutting class, the seventh grade will be demoted one grade in behavior for the first quarter. This will go on homeroom teacher Margarita Ivanovna's record. The parents will be informed . . ."

We heard the buses pulling into the school parking lot, and a bell went off in the school—the signal to leave. We jumped to grab our luggage. But Margarita Ivanovna said calmly, "Take your seats."

Everyone crawled back into their seats, but for some reason I sat down on my suitcase. Naturally I fell and it fell. And then other suitcases fell. It made a lot of noise.

"Bessoltseva, stop clowning," Margarita Ivanovna said.

"I'm not clowning," I said. I really wasn't, Grandfather.

We could hear feet running down the hallways and the stairs, and voices making happy noises, running past our doors. Someone stuck his head in and yelled, "Why are you sitting there? The buses are ready!"

Red couldn't stand it. "Margarita Ivanovna, won't we miss the bus?" he asked politely.

"You won't miss it," Margarita Ivanovna replied, "because you're not going anywhere!"

Not going to Moscow!

Red was horrified. "What do you mean, we're not going?"

Popov jumped up and took two suitcases, his and Shmakova's. "We didn't go to the movies! Shmakova and I didn't do anything wrong!"

"But you didn't show up for class, either. So no one is going anywhere!"

Popov stood there with the suitcases, looking stupid. "Put down the suitcases!" Shmakova ordered.

Suddenly Vasiliev laughed.

"What's so funny?" Margarita Ivanovna asked.

"I've figured it out—you're kidding."

"Kidding? Why should I be kidding?"

"Why else would you be wearing your new dress?" Vasiliev asked, laughing again, nervously.

"I'm wearing my new dress because I am going to Moscow," said Margarita Ivanovna. "You're the ones who aren't going."

Vasiliev's face fell. "That's not fair," he said. "You got chewed out by the principal, and now you're going and we're not."

Margarita Ivanovna got even angrier. "Well, let me explain something to you," she said. "I didn't run off to the movies. I got into trouble because of *you*. I was supposed to leave for Moscow earlier, but I postponed my trip. And why did I postpone my trip? So that I could help you find work and earn money for the trip, so that I could give you all an extra credit, to prove what an extraordinary class I had. People in Moscow were upset with me . . ."

We all knew who in Moscow was upset with her: her fiancé. When she mentioned her fiancé and the extra grades, Iron Button jumped up, all pale, and said very calmly, "We don't need your 'extra credit.' You should have gone earlier, then no one would have been upset with you."

Margarita Ivanovna's eyes almost popped out.

42

"Aren't you ashamed of yourselves?"

"Why should we be ashamed?" Val asked. "We didn't steal anything."

"Do you think stealing is the only thing to be ashamed of?"

"What else is there?" Val asked. "We didn't break any laws."

Then everyone started shouting, furious at Margarita Ivanovna and themselves: "We don't want to go to Moscow!"

"We want more D's!"

"Then we have nothing more to talk about," said Margarita Ivanovna, heading for the door.

"Margarita Ivanovna, wait!" Dimka tried to stop her. "They're just kidding. We worked to earn money for this trip! I'll go to the principal and explain everything. Honest, we'll never do it again. Margarita Ivanovna, may I go to the principal?" He pressed his back against the door and wouldn't let her out. "You can punish us later, Margarita Ivanovna."

"Move away from the door, Somov!" Margarita Ivanovna said. "It's too late now."

"What will we do with the money?" Dimka asked.

Margarita Ivanovna spun on her heels, slowly walked over to her desk, picked up the bank, raised it high over her head, and—smashed it on the floor! It was like a volcano erupting.

"You can go to the movies every day now," she said, and left.

"Let's divide up the money and party!" Val shouted.

Vasiliev tried to stop them, but Shaggy pushed him aside and said, "Divide it up, Shmakova!" Shmakova picked up the money, brought it to the table, and started counting.

"Boy, that's a lot of money!" Val was salivating, as if it were some delicious food instead of money on the table.

"Don't touch it!" Dimka shouted. He started stuffing the money into his pockets, saying, "We'll go to Moscow for winter vacation."

Val grabbed him, shouting that the money belonged to everyone and Dimka was trying to rob them. Shaggy and Red came to Val's assistance. They twisted Dimka's arms behind his back and started pulling the money out of his pockets. Dimka looked really pathetic.

"Divide it up, Shmakova!" Shaggy said.

"Shmakova, don't!" Dimka could barely breathe. "Don't listen to Shaggy!"

"Don't be bossy, Dimka," Shmakova sang sweetly. "I'm not Bessoltseva, you know." She narrowed her eyes and watched Dimka. "You're so honest and decisive. Our brave leader." I told you, Grandfather, she's a real fox—singing in a sweet voice like a lullaby while she hits you in the solar plexus. Dimka sat there like a beaten dog. I felt sorry for him.

Shmakova counted the money, her lips moving, sounding like leaves rustling in the grass. "There! Fair and square! Everybody gets twenty-three rubles." Thirty-six piles lay on the teacher's desk—one for each member of the class. "Well, what are you gaping at? Come and get it!"

Shmakova neatly picked up one pile. "I'll add to this and get myself a blue jacket I saw in the department store. It's gorgeous!"

Val was next to grab his money—he counted it.

"Don't you trust me?" Shmakova asked.

"Money likes to be counted," Val replied.

The others started taking their money. Some grabbed it, some took it casually, some counted it. Shaggy took two piles and brought one to Mironova. Only Dimka's money and mine remained on the desk.

"What's the matter, don't you want your money?" Shmakova asked, looking very smug and pleased with herself, as if she knew something no one else did.

"They're altruists," joked Val.

Dimka was standing next to me, and I could feel him shaking. He walked over to the desk, took his money, and shouted, "Lousy money grubbers! I hope you choke on it!" He walked over to Val. "Here! Take it!" He thrust the money at him.

I was glad to see him in control again, and I shouted, "Give him mine too!"

Dimka kept thrusting the money at Val and it fell on the floor, scattering, because Val was backing away from him, pushing him away with his hands and muttering, "Get away from me, you psycho!"

Vasiliev shouted that we should give all the money back to Dimka so we could go to Moscow in the winter.

"Right!" Dimka said. "Put the money here!" He picked bills up off the floor and piled them back on the teacher's desk.

I was bursting with pride, and I thought this would be a good time for him to tell them about Margarita Ivanovna. That he had told her everything not out of cowardice, but because he believed in telling the truth.

I was running around the classroom saying, "Give him your money, come on, come on, give it back!" when Iron Button shouted above the general noise.

"Stop gabbing, Somov," she said. "You keep foaming at the mouth about the money, but we need to find out something much more important."

"Did you hear what she said, guys?" Dimka's eyes were glimmering. "I'm suggesting we save our money for winter vacation and she calls that gabbing! Dear Iron Button, if I'm gabbing, what do you consider important?" He put his hand to his ear. "I'm anxious to hear."

I put my hand to my ear and repeated, "Tell us, dear Iron Button, what do you consider important?"

Iron Button didn't move a muscle. "Gang!" she shouted, ignoring us completely. "Do you know what's important? I do. Someone snitched to Margarita Ivanovna. One of us is a traitor."

When I heard her say that I looked at Dimka. I wanted to cry out, "Speak out or it'll be too late!" But my tongue turned to stone. And Dimka remained silent. All the kids were shouting, furiously: "We'll find the snitch!"

"We'll get him!"

"There's a snake in the grass here!"

"You mean one of us snitched?" Shaggy shouted.

"Yes," Mironova said.

"Who?" asked Shaggy.

It grew quiet. They were waiting for Iron Button to tell them who it was. She looked at everyone in turn. Her eyes were piercing as they moved slowly over our faces.

When she got to Dimka she said in a strange

47

voice, "Dimka . . . you went back. . . ."

Her manner of stretching words out upset me. I sat there trembling.

"Right!" Shaggy grabbed Dimka by the front of the shirt. "You went back! Fess up! Did you snitch to Margarita Ivanovna?"

"He's got a conscience," Val said, sneering. "He could have told her."

"The important thing is strength, not conscience!" Shaggy raised a huge fist above Dimka's head. "If I punch you on the head, your feet will come flying off!"

"Oooh," sang Shmakova, "Dimka is scared. Gang, our brave Dimka is scared. What a laugh!" And she shook with laughter.

Dimka pulled away from Shaggy.

"Somov's hiding something!" Val shouted. "Look at him, his eyes are shifty. He's weaseling out!"

"Bug off!" Dimka cried out in a strange voice. "I'm sick of you. We didn't go to Moscow because of you! 'We want the movies! We want the movies!' And look where it got you." Dimka headed for the door and I followed.

"I know who the traitor is," Iron Button said in a very casual way, with this little smile of hers.

Dimka and I stopped dead in our tracks. I was sure she was going to name Dimka. Voices came from every side: "Who? Who? Who?" Shaggy hopped over to Mironova. "Tell us, who is it?"

I took a look at Dimka—he was unrecognizable. His blue eyes had turned white. White! He had this pathetic little smile, sort of like mine. And my lips stretched out in response to it. A fine pair we made! Then it came to me in a flash. I guessed what had made Dimka look like that: Fear! When I saw that he was afraid, for some reason, I stopped being afraid. I took his hand in mine and squeezed hard. I wanted him to know he wasn't alone. I thought he understood and sort of nodded at me. And I saw that his eyes were back to being blue, and that made me happy.

Everyone was waiting to see what would happen next. Iron Button was in no hurry to reveal her secret.

"Come on, Mironova, don't drag it out!" said Red.

She did drag it out, longer and longer. "Let's give him three minutes to think about it," she said finally, looking at her watch.

"One minute!" Shmakova called in her foxy voice.

A creepy silence filled those three minutes as everyone tried to figure out who the traitor was.

"If he doesn't confess, it'll be worse for him," Mironova said nastily. "Well!" she shouted, and it was like a whip being cracked. "Come on, confess! If you admit it, things will go easier for you!"

"Popov," Shmakova ordered, "go stand by the door, so *he* doesn't escape." And she laughed.

"Two minutes!" Mironova said, almost without opening her lips.

I looked at Dimka—he stood there, dumbstruck. "Dimka," I whispered, trying to nudge him. I wanted to scream at him, hit him, make him move, make him confess before Iron Button named him.

"Three!" snapped Mironova's voice.

"Three! Three! Three!" rang in my head. Things swam before my eyes, and I would have fallen if Popov hadn't caught me.

When I came to, I realized that Dimka hadn't confessed; he was still standing next to me and no one was paying much attention to us.

"Well?" Shaggy rushed to Mironova. "Who is it?"

And here Dimka whispered, "Hey . . ."

Shmakova was the only one who heard him. "Quiet, everyone! Dimka wants to tell us something!" she said in her singsongy voice.

But then Iron Button did something that changed the whole situation. "Come to me one at a time," she ordered. "I'll measure your pulse. We'll see how fast the traitor's heart is beating!"

"So you don't know who it is?" Dimka asked hoarsely. I saw how relieved and happy he was. He had been given a reprieve.

"Maybe someone else knows?" Popov said, grinning broadly.

"*No one* else knows, my dear Popov," said Shmakova, and she stared hard at Popov. "And we won't rush. . . ." She was practically dancing in the aisles, and singing, "We'll learn everything in time. Who it is . . . and what he told Margarita Ivanovna . . . and why he did it. . . ."

"Come to me one at a time," Iron Button said.

Vasiliev was first. "Go ahead," he said, giving her his hand.

Mironova began counting Vasiliev's pulse. The rest watched in silence. "Normal," Mironova said. "Next!"

One by one everyone in the class let Mironova measure their pulse.

After Shmakova, Iron Button took Popov's pulse. That left only two people—Dimka and me! But Iron Button dropped Popov's hand, her cheeks had turned crimson, and she said, "Pulse—one hundred!"

"Pulse one hundred! Pulse one hundred!" went up and down the rows.

"What's normal?" Shaggy asked.

"Seventy!" Iron Button looked around the class triumphantly.

"You louse!" Shaggy grabbed Popov and twisted his arm.

"He and Shmakova didn't go to the movies with us," Red shouted. "I bet they planned to go to Moscow alone."

The kids surrounded Popov and started yelling at him.

"Leave Popov alone," Dimka said calmly. I was sure he was going to tell them. I began shivering with fright, but he had no intention of confessing. "Margarita Ivanovna would have found out anyway," he said. "It was our own fault, there's no point in looking for a scapegoat. What difference does it make whether it was Popov or someone else?"

"It makes a big difference," Iron Button said angrily. "Do you know what happens to traitors? Come on, Popov, talk!"

Popov grinned and looked at Shmakova. "Why not? I'll talk!"

"Some people won't like that," Shmakova said with a smile. "But what can you do! You can't please everyone."

Popov was glowing. "Here's what happened." he said, and gave Dimka a look that made me think he knew! I looked over at Dimka, and I could tell that he was terrified. So I rushed to help him out.

"Listen!" I shouted. "Listen to me!"

Iron Button was annoyed. "Why are you bothering us?"

"She's not bothering," Shmakova said, and looked at me strangely. "Maybe she knows something. Talk, Bessoltseva! We're waiting impatiently."

"Kids," I said, "it was . . . it was . . ."

I stared at Dimka, hoping he would understand the time had come to admit his guilt. But he was silent.

"It was . . ." I decided to name him myself, since he couldn't. But I stopped, I just couldn't do it.

Shmakova stood there in a triumphant pose, arms crossed over her chest. "Well, talk. Who do you think did it?" she sang sweetly.

Grandfather! I looked at Shmakova and knew she'd be thrilled if I named Dimka. And suddenly for some reason I smiled at her and said something completely different from what I had planned. . . .

"It was me!"

"So that's what happened!" *Lena* had taken the blame! Nikolai Nikolayevich had never even considered this possibility. Lena was a true Bessoltsev, truly caring for other people. He got up and crossed the room, humming to himself, something he did very rarely.

"What's the matter with you?" Lena asked, bewildered.

"Nothing." Nikolai Nikolayevich smiled quite happily. "Absolutely nothing! Go on, child, go on."

Everyone thought I was joking. I looked again at Dimka, smiled, and repeated it loudly: "I did it! It was me!"

Their faces were so funny! Red's mouth fell open.

"You!" cried Shmakova.

Popov stared at me in disbelief.

Vasiliev looked confused. "That's impossible!" he finally said.

"It's true, it's true!" I shouted. "I did it!" I looked at Dimka; I wanted him to come forward and confess.

Vasiliev leaned over to me and whispered, "I get it—you're pulling their legs?"

I laughed, and Vasiliev, looking even more confused, laughed too.

Iron Button looked at me, her face growing hard. "What made you do it, you miserable scarecrow?" she asked.

"I just did," I replied cheerfully. "I ran to

the nurse's office to have my knee bandaged, I saw Margarita Ivanovna, and . . . I told her everything." I looked at Dimka again, but he didn't respond.

Shaggy hit me between the shoulder blades with the side of his hand, but I didn't even flinch.

Vasiliev winked at me and said, "Boy, she's brave! Shaggy, she's not afraid of you!"

I really wasn't afraid. Something had happened to me. I didn't even recognize myself—it was like being someone else.

Anyway, as soon as I had confessed, Iron Button ordered the door shut. Val shoved the teacher's chair under the doorknob and rubbed his hands in glee. "This is going to be fun!"

We were locked in—alone, all alone in this room.

No one knew what to do next.

Val threw an eraser at me, which hit the wall and bounced off Popov's face. "Why hit me?" Popov whined.

It was like a comic relief, and everyone laughed. I laughed too, and winked at Dimka: *Aren't you having fun?*

But Dimka was glummer than glum.

Iron Button did not laugh either. She jumped up on a desk and said, "There is a traitor among us!" Her cheeks were red with outrage. "What are we going to do with her?"

Val shouted, "Burn her at the stake!"

"Right!" Red said. "Burn her at the stake!" Everyone laughed again. I laughed too, and looked at Dimka.

But Iron Button did not join in. "Shaggy," she said, "smack Red for goofing around."

Red got angry. He ran over to me and spat out, "You bitch!"

"All right, Red, shut up for now. And drop the funny stuff," Iron Button ordered. "We have to make a serious decision here. Are we going to forgive her?" Her eyes practically turned everyone to ashes.

Everyone started shouting: "We won't!"

"We will!"

And for some reason I joined in: "Don't forgive! Don't!"

"Quiet!" Iron Button snapped.

Mironova knew that everyone was waiting to hear what she had to say next, so she dragged it out. "I declare a boycott against Bessoltseva!"

"Yes, a boycott! Boy-cott!"

Just then someone pulled at the door from the outside, and we heard Margarita Ivanovna's voice.

I was afraid she would burst in and give Dimka away. But he was more scared than me. He tiptoed over to the door and put his fingers to his lips: *Be quiet!* Like a fool, I did the same thing.

"Open the door this instant!" Margarita Ivanovna cried.

Dimka was white as a sheet.

"Open this door!"

Iron Button pushed Dimka aside and opened the door.

"What boycott?" Margarita Ivanovna demanded. "What's going on here?"

We were silent.

And then somebody called out from the hall, "Margarita Ivanovna! Margarita Ivanovna! A call from Moscow for you!"

Margarita Ivanovna looked around distractedly and left the room.

Iron Button calmly shut the door and said, "So, what do we do to Bessoltseva?"

Cries of "Boycott!" came from every direction.

"No one, do you hear me, not a single person," Iron Button pronounced, "may say a word to her. Anyone who breaks this vow will also be boycotted!"

"This will be fun. Right, Somov?" Val said. "We'll give your girlfriend a rough time. Boycott the scarecrow!"

Dimka smiled wryly and said nothing.

But everyone else had something to say. "What? Is Somov against the boycott?"

"Somov's breaking ranks!"

"No good, Somov!"

"What's the matter, Dimka?" Shmakova asked sweetly. "Aren't you with us?"

Dimka was still smiling, but I could tell he didn't feel like it. Val kept pestering him, tugging at him, prodding him. "Come on, come on, let's say it together: Boycott the scarecrow!"

He was getting a good rhythm in the chant.

I couldn't stand it any longer; I felt sorry for Dimka and shouted right in Val's face, "Boy-cott! . . . Boy-cott!"

Val recoiled. "Are you crazy?"

Outside, the parking lot had come to life — the drivers had turned on the engines of the buses. "The buses are leaving!" Shmakova shouted.

We rushed to the windows and stared with envy at the school parking lot.

"Look, there's Margarita Ivanovna with a bouquet. She sure looks happy," Shmakova said. "A bride!"

"She's looking this way! Smile at her. Smile, I said," Iron Button ordered, smiling. "Now wave." She waved to Margarita Ivanovna. "I don't want the old witch to think we've rolled over and died of grief."

"They're leaving!" Red said, his voice quivering. "And I'm stuck here!" There were tears in his eyes.

"What was Dimka doing all this time?" Nikolai Nikolayevich interrupted, practically shouting.

"Dimka? Nothing. He turned away from me so I wouldn't catch his eye."

Then Margarita Ivanovna waved to us. And Shmakova said, "What's she waving for?"

"Hey, she's calling us!" Red shouted like a madman. "She's changed her mind!"

They all rushed out of the classroom, and Dimka and I were left alone. He looked at me in a way he'd never looked at me before. He was so sad. I think he wanted to say something, something important. And I could see the words were on the tip of his tongue and everything would have been different. But I laughed. Can you imagine? I laughed!

And so he ran away from me. I followed him.

Lena was quiet again. Nikolai Nikolayevich saw the corners of her mouth droop, and he knew she was remembering something very unpleasant.

"Grandfather, will I ever be happy again?" Lena asked suddenly.

"Don't be silly, child. Of course you will!"

But Nikolai Nikolayevich was very concerned. "You'll be happy again, you'll see" he said kindly.

Lena sat on the couch, her feet curled up under her. Her knees were against Nikolai Nikolayevich's side, and he could feel her trembling. *Poor girl, it hit her really hard,* he thought, *and tenderly covered her with a blanket.*

By the time Dimka and I got to the school yard, everyone was singing and dancing. The buses roared, parents were waving good-bye to their children. Only our class stood there in a silent huddle. Like a motionless iceberg in a roiling sea.

Then the teachers who weren't going to Moscow came out to see Margarita Ivanovna off to her wedding. Margarita Ivanovna laughed, kissed, and hugged — and suddenly she noticed us! The smile flew from her lips and she headed toward us, the large bouquet of flowers in her arms.

"So what's this business about a boycott?" Margarita Ivanovna asked me.

"Boycott?" Iron Button asked. "Oh, the boycott!" She gave me a look that said, *Just try to tell her, you miserable scarecrow.*

"Oh, Margarita Ivanovna, you've spilled something on your beautiful dress!" Shmakova chimed in.

Margarita Ivanovna ignored her. "I didn't ask you, Mironova," she said. "I was talking to Bessoltseva. Well, Bessoltseva. Why are you being boycotted?"

I couldn't reply. I could see Margarita Ivanovna's thoughts were with her fiancé in Moscow. She looked so happy and radiant and it made me feel happy too.

"Well, talk, Bessoltseva. Why are you being boycotted?"

I could feel Shaggy's fist in my ribs, and that made me laugh. "It's just a game," I said.

"Why are you laughing, Bessoltseva?" Margarita Ivanovna was annoyed. "I don't see any reason for you to be laughing."

"I'm ticklish," I explained.

"Ticklish? Who's tickling you? What is this nonsense?" That really upset her. "This is ridiculous! You're all behaving outlandishly. When I get back, I'll get to the bottom of this, I definitely will!"

Just then one of the teachers shouted through a megaphone, "Margarita Ivanovna! You'll be late for your wedding!"

Margarita Ivanovna stared at me for a minute longer; then she turned and ran for the bus.

The buses moved slowly and smoothly past

us. Somebody waved to us, somebody else made a mean face. We could see smiling Margarita Ivanovna settling down in the front seat with her flowers.

The school parking lot was empty except for us and the first graders. Slowly and sadly we headed back to the classroom to pick up our luggage. Iron Button's gang surrounded me. Their eyes were angry, mean, alien. They were all against me!

I think I shuddered.

And then it began. . . .

"You snake in the grass!" Val shouted. "Look what your hissing has done!" he yelled.

"Brownnose!"

"Traitor!"

"Snitch!"

Dimka tried to stop them. "What's wrong with you guys? We didn't decide anything!"

"Yes, we did," Iron Button snapped.

"Bessoltseva, tell them. Tell them you were joking," Vasiliev pleaded.

"No jokes, right, Dimka?" Shmakova sang.

Dimka did not reply.

"Burn her at the stake!" Red shouted.

"I told you, I told you! He's on her side!" Val shouted gleefully. "You'll pay for this, Somov!"

"Make a circle!" Iron Button ordered. "Hold

your hands tight, so they can't escape."

They held hands and the circle turned into a wheel that was going to run over Dimka and me.

"Now, why is it that Somov is against the boycott, and we let him get away with it?" Val demanded. "Let's boycott Somov too!"

"Shut up!" Iron Button entered the circle, ignoring me altogether, and asked Dimka, "Somov, are you against boycotting Bessoltseva?"

Dimka looked at me and said nothing.

"He doesn't answer. That means he's against it!" Red shouted.

"Then we boycott him too!" Iron Button declared.

"Me?" Dimka was scared. "Boycott me?"

Val laughed with glee.

"From this minute on, Somov, you no longer exist for us," Iron Button said.

"Now you see him, now you don't!" Shmakova sang.

"Mironova, listen," Dimka pleaded. But she turned away from him.

"Shmakova, are you against me too?"

"I don't go around with traitors," sang Shmakova.

"Let's beat them up!" yelled Shaggy.

I shut my eyes.

Vasiliev broke the circle and grabbed Shaggy

before he could get to us. Dimka pulled me by the hand and we ran.

We could hear footsteps behind us. They were closing in on us. I could recognize their voices: "After them!" That was Mironova.

"Beat them up!" That was Val.

And Shmakova sang out, "Boycott!"

We stopped by the beauty parlor for a rest. I was almost happy. I had saved Dimka; now he was saving me.

Mrs. Klava, the beautician and Red's mother, looked out the door. She saw us, smiled.

Suddenly Dimka turned to me and asked, "When did you have time to tell Margarita Ivanovna?"

"Me? . . . Margarita Ivanovna?" I couldn't go on. Was he so stupid that he could think that *I* snitched, that he didn't realize I was taking the blame for him? I looked in the beauty parlor mirror and sort of sang, for some reason, "Margarita-a-a!"

"Answer me!"

"Mar-ga-ri-ta-ta-ta-ta!" I sang, and sort of danced. "Did you notice her eyes? She was talking to us, but she saw only her fiancé. And her dress! Wasn't it gorgeous? When I grow up, I'll have one like that."

Dimka was getting agitated. "Stop gibbering. Tell me when you told her."

"I didn't tell her!"

I looked in the mirror again and thought that I looked okay when my mouth was shut. Dimka was behind me, but in the mirror our faces were next to each other. I liked looking at the two of us — it was like being in a photograph together.

"Then who did you tell?" Dimka persisted.

"Nobody!" I kept my mouth shut and smiled so I didn't look like Big Mouth.

"What do you mean, nobody?"

"Nobody!" I turned slowly, made my eyes really big, and kept my lips together.

"Then why did you tell the gang that you did it?"

"I just did." I smiled beautifully again. "I wasn't planning to at first. I was going to tell them it was you. But then something inside made me open my mouth and say, 'I did it!' "

He stared at me in disbelief.

"What are you staring at?" I said, and then added slowly, "I was outside the door when you spoke to Margarita Ivanovna, and heard everything."

He stared in disbelief. "You did it for *me*?"

"No," I said, "I did it for William Shakespeare."

"I don't believe it. You did it for me? What are you going to do now?"

"Whatever you want." I was happy he finally

realized I had saved him.

"They'll hound us to death," Dimka said glumly.

"I'm not afraid," I replied. "We're together, aren't we?"

Suddenly he jolted like a madman. "Let's go back! I'll tell them the truth! I'll tell them I did it."

"Here's your chance, here they come," I said when I noticed them turning the corner, with Iron Button in the lead.

But instead of facing the gang, Dimka covered my mouth with his hand and dragged me through the open door of the beauty parlor. We hid behind the curtain.

Mrs. Klava looked at us with surprise. She clearly wanted to know what was going on, but didn't have time to ask because Mironova, Shaggy, Red, Val, Shmakova, and Popov appeared outside the window.

If I hadn't been a fool, I would have known from the beginning that he was too much of a coward to confess. But I was blind. I looked at Dimka, and I saw that his eyes were darting around, his lips trembling. . . . That's why I felt sorry for him. When no one was around, he was brave, but in the presence of the gang, he was the lowest of cowards.

In this trembling, quivering voice he begged

Mrs. Klava, "Please don't tell them we're here. It's a game."

Mrs. Klava nodded, opened the door, and shouted, "Tolya! Why didn't you go to Moscow?"

"They didn't take us," Red replied. I never knew his real name was Tolya.

When Red told her why we weren't taken on the trip to Moscow, she covered her face with her hands. "Oh, no! And I called your father. He's expecting you."

"Expecting me?" I saw Red's face change. His cheeks were blazing. "Expecting me?"

"Of course." Mrs. Klava ran her fingers through his hair. "He wants to see you."

I glanced over at Dimka — it wasn't right to eavesdrop. I nudged him to come out, but he pushed me back against the wall.

"Maybe he'll come here?" Red asked softly and uncertainly.

Mrs. Klava sighed. "He can't come here."

"Why not?" I had never heard Red sound so sad and desperate. "I haven't seen him in three years!"

"He won't come here." Mrs. Klava sighed again.

"He will! He will!" Red shouted.

I could see Mrs. Klava embrace him. "Don't cry, Tolya! Please don't cry. You'll see him another time."

"Hey, Red!" Shaggy called from the street. "They're not here. Let's go!"

"I'll get even with them!" Red pulled away from his mother. "I'll let that scarecrow have it!"

"Tolya! Tolya!" Mrs. Klava called, but Red was gone.

Mrs. Klava came back into the beauty parlor and bumped into us—she had forgotten we were there. "Wait a minute—aren't you in my Tolya's class?" she said.

"Yes," Dimka admitted.

"How could you! Shameless kids!" Mrs. Klava shook her head and sobbed.

Dimka put his arm around my shoulder and we ran out of the beauty parlor, right into Dimka's sister, nasty Svetka. "Dimka has a girlfriend! Dimka has a girlfriend!" she started chanting.

"Stupid!" Dimka said. "Don't pay any attention to her."

But I looked at Svetka and forgot my plan to be beautiful at all times and smiled my Big Mouth smile and said, "Say it again."

"Dimka has a girlfriend!" she sang out, and ran off.

You know, Grandfather, I liked her calling me his girlfriend. I felt so good. And I wanted to do something special, so I turned to Dimka and said, "I'm going to get my hair done! I'm sick of these braids."

"That's a great idea," he said. "I'll come with you."

So we turned around and ran back inside the beauty parlor.

"Did Dimka say anything about the gang?" Nikolai Nikolayevich was practically shouting.

"He told me, 'I think the gang won't believe me if I confess now. They'll think I'm just trying to save you. I'd better do it alone.' "

"Well, well!" Nikolai Nikolayevich said. "This is getting very interesting. What did you tell him?"

"I said, 'I think what you think!' "

"Clever!" said Nikolai Nikolayevich. "What did he do?"

"He was so quiet. I think he liked my words, and that made me happy. That meant I had helped him out once more."

"Fine knight he is!" Nikolai Nikolayevich was incensed. "You get beaten and knocked around, and he does nothing but think of his own skin. What a sweet, sweet boy, so thoughtful and kind!"

"Do you think I was wrong to feel sorry for Dimka?" asked Lena.

"Personally I don't like scoundrels," said Nikolai Nikolayevich.

"He's not a scoundrel! He's not! He wasn't a scoundrel yet!" Lena replied. She began whispering. "I couldn't have done anything different then. . . . I'm glad I helped him."

"Then why do you want to leave now?" asked Nikolai Nikolayevich.

Lena looked at him like a cornered mouse.

But Nikolai Nikolayevich couldn't stop. "You're not kind at all! Dimka's the only one you forgive. What about the others?"

"The others are mean!" Lena shouted. "Evil! They're wolves and foxes, that's what! He would have confessed a long time ago if they were different."

"I don't believe everyone in your class is mean!" Nikolai Nikolayevich said. "That's impossible."

"You don't believe me?" Lena asked softly, and looked up at him, hoping not to find confirmation of those words in his eyes.

Nikolai Nikolayevich shook his head. He was ready to take back his words out of pity for her, but on the other hand, what good would it do? She might run to the scoundrel and forgive him again!

"They're *all* horrible!" Lena shouted.

"I'll never believe that!" Nikolai Nikolayevich said. "Never!"

71

"You don't know the whole story and you're against me already!" Lena cringed. "I don't want to see you ever again! I'm leaving!" She got up off the couch.

Nikolai Nikolayevich grabbed her by the shoulder. He thought she would struggle, but she turned to him and her face, which had just been furious, was sensitive and helpless, as if she were eight years old.

"All right, let's calm down." Nikolai Nikolayevich held her close, felt her warm neck. Her neck was a thin reed, a straw. "Let's sit down." He pulled Lena down with him and sat her on the couch. "Tell me the whole story. You're right, I'm jumping to conclusions. . . ." He hugged her, feeling the sharp bones of her shoulders.

Lena said nothing.

Nikolai Nikolayevich tried to joke with her, tell her funny stories, but nothing helped. Lena huddled in the corner of the couch, silent. Nikolai Nikolayevich sighed deeply, put on his jacket, and went outside.

He brought in an armload of firewood and dumped it on the floor, breaking the unnatural silence.

But Lena said nothing.

He lit a fire, and the heat went up in a fiery column. The potbellied black stove crackled and trembled with the heat.

Nikolai Nikolayevich thought the heat was strong enough to break through the roof and shoot up into the sky like a rocket. Maybe it would carry Lena's sadness up to the eternal stars, to the moon, to the sun?

But nothing like that happened. The fire gradually died down, first with bright red, then with glowing blue coals.

Nikolai Nikolayevich was completely confused. He didn't know what to do about Lena's misery.

Then he lit the other stoves and wandered from room to room, looking at the family portraits. The elongated, stern faces and large eyes silently watched Nikolai Nikolayevich bend over the stoves and toss in logs, not letting the fires go out.

If his ancestor had not painted these portraits, and if other Bessoltsevs, from generation to generation, had not saved them, no one would have known that these people ever lived, he thought. Nikolai Nikolayevich suddenly felt very old.

As he added logs to the fires, he recalled waking up one morning and feeling that he had always lived here. He belonged here with the Bessoltsev family's past.

He went from portrait to portrait, silently talking to each one, until he reached *Mashka.*

He looked over at Lena—they looked so much alike. In the portrait Mashka stood in a doorway, translucently white, in a homespun, floor-length shirt, her head shaven. Had she been ill? Her mouth was half open, as if she were about to say something to him. That was why he always approached Mashka softly.

Nikolai Nikolayevich remembered how Lena had been drawn to *Mashka* the day the painting arrived. He had heard her say to it, "Don't look at me like that." But when he asked her about it, Lena blushed and said nothing. Then, later, early one morning, he heard Lena singing. The strange thing was that it sounded as if two people were singing.

"Who are you singing with?" he had asked.

Lena laughed and said, "With Mashka!"

All that was in the past, the dear, sweet past, which was ruined, soured forever. He *had* to help Lena get out of her vicious circle.

Nikolai Nikolayevich went upstairs and out onto each of the four balconies, the way Lena liked to do. He looked in all four directions, hoping one of them would help. But nothing helped.

He went out into the yard. He began sawing off dried branches from trees and covering the fresh wounds with brown paint. He thought that might attract Lena—she liked to dip the brush into the paint and stroke the light wood of the cut, making a bright spot on the gray trunk. But Lena didn't come out to help. Things were really bad!

Finally Lena came outside, and Nikolai Nikolayevich started shadowing her. Wherever she went, he went. He wanted to pluck a word from her silent lips, talk to her, make her laugh. But she was silent.

He looked into her sad, frightened eyes, and it was like a stab to his heart. He wanted so much to help her, he wanted to ease her pain. He made a move toward her, but Lena walked past him, her head standing out against the rain-wet branches.

Nikolai Nikolayevich went back inside the house and lay down on his bed, pulling the blanket over his head, hoping for a little rest, hoping to wake up with a firm and definite plan of how to help Lena.

He slept briefly and badly. He imagined someone was calling him softly, pulling his nose. He opened his eyes — and there was Lena. Nikolai Nikolayevich blinked, shut his eyes, opened them, and no one was there. Vanished.

Nikolai Nikolayevich turned over and just as he was falling asleep he heard his name again.

He woke up worried: Where was Lena?

He crept over to her room. Lena was asleep,

her face peaceful, almost saintly.

And that pathetic, vile Dimka Somov rejected such a beautiful and wonderful soul! thought Nikolai Nikolayevich angrily.

Slowly and quietly he moved across the room, holding his breath so as not to wake Lena. At the doorway he turned. Lena was looking back at him, her eyes half open. She was watching him like a cat about to pounce on a mouse, not letting on that she was watching.

"I dreamed that someone pulled my nose," Nikolai Nikolayevich said apologetically, hoping that would make her laugh.

It worked. "Your nose?" Lena laughed.

"And I dreamed that the person tweaking my nose was you!"

"Me?" Lena laughed again.

Nikolai Nikolayevich liked it when she laughed like that, like a glass bell that rang as it fell in the grass.

"Maybe you did come to my room?" Nikolai Nikolayevich asked cautiously.

Lena nodded.

"And tweaked my nose?"

Lena nodded again.

"Outrageous! How dare you! You could have left me noseless! Or scratched me, which is also not pleasant."

"I wanted to wake you. You know why?" She

looked as if she were about to reveal a great secret. "You were right. I'm not kind at all. Remember when I told you Red is like a circus clown? All the kids laughed at him, and I did too, and he laughed at himself, Grandfather — there were tears in his eyes when he laughed! Grandfather, what if he wasn't laughing, but crying? What if the tears were tears of pain? Maybe I was wrong about him."

"Maybe you were wrong about someone else too?" Nikolai Nikolayevich asked softly.

"You think so?" Lena thought hard. "Who?"

Lena's mobile face changed rapidly, it took on a bewildered expression, the corners of her mouth dropped. She turned to Nikolai Nikolaye-vich, and he saw her large, sad eyes in the pink-ish-gray light of the fading day.

Dimka waited for me outside the beauty parlor. When he saw Mironova and Shmakova, he instinctively ran around the corner to hide from them. He told me that he was about to come out of hiding and face the gang, when he remembered he hadn't told his parents that the trip to Moscow was canceled. So he decided to run home to tell them.

On the way home it occurred to him that he should have told me where he was going. What if I came out of the beauty parlor and he wasn't there. Instead, there would be Iron Button's gang, taunting and hitting me—they were capable of that. So he turned back, only to bump into Val.

"Where's your girlfriend?" Val asked.

"How am I supposed to know?" Dimka burst out. "You're the one who's stalking her, not me." He started for home again, imagining how he would confess his "betrayal" to the gang. Wouldn't they all laugh! They would forgive him. He could persuade them that he had been right. He would tell them that I wanted to help him because I liked him and thought he was afraid. And he kept quiet because he wanted to build up my will power.

He liked the idea a lot, it sounded convincing, so Dimka headed back to the beauty parlor.

But then he stopped and decided he could do it later—he had to tell his parents about the trip, and he headed back home. And he stopped again: *What if the gang catches Lena and starts terrorizing her?* he thought. *Ah, they won't do anything to her,* he consoled himself. *They're probably all home eating lunch.*

Dimka felt hungry, remembered they were having chicken and noodles for lunch, and hurried home.

But the gang had no thoughts of lunch. Mironova and Shmakova were standing near the beauty parlor, waiting for the rest of the gang, who were looking for us. I was inside having my hair done.

"They must be somewhere," I heard Shmakova say.

"We'll get them," Iron Button said grimly.

"My poor feet," Shmakova complained. "I got up at six this morning. Woke the whole house.

Packed. Washed my hair. Mother had a new dress ready for me. And gave me some money without my father knowing. She's sweet. We made a long shopping list. What were you planning to buy in Moscow?"

"Nothing," Iron Button said through clenched teeth.

"Why are you like that, Mironova?" Shmakova asked Iron Button.

"Like what?"

"Not like other girls. Your mother is so chic. She's the woman of my dreams."

"That figures," Iron Button said with a sneer.

"I saw your mother yesterday," said Shmakova. "She was wearing a blue leather jacket that matched her eyes. It was gorgeous! It must have cost a bundle?"

"I wouldn't know, Shmakova. Let's talk about something else."

"All right, but don't get mad. Tell me, Iron Button, you're so honest and righteous, so why are you against Scarecrow? What did Scarecrow do that was so bad? All she did was tell Margarita Ivanovna what happened. She told the truth. And you want to punish her for that! Is that right?"

"She betrayed us," said Iron Button. "She thought no one would find out. She 'told the truth,' as you put it. But there are different kinds of truth. Her truth is betrayal."

"You're very principled," Shmakova said.

"And why are you against Bessoltseva?" asked Mironova.

"I have my own ax to grind," said Shmakova.

"That's rather petty."

"To each his own," said Shmakova.

Shmakova likes knowing more than everyone else, and she waited patiently, gloating. She had enjoyed watching Dimka squirm when Iron Button had announced she knew who the snitch was. Or when he thought Margarita Ivanovna would tell the class.

"I have an ax to grind with everyone." Iron Button's eyes blazed with indignation. "If you don't live by the truth—there's retribution! No one must go unpunished. Never!" Then she added, almost in a whisper, "Even family."

"Yup, you have principles!" Shmakova laughed for some reason.

"They're not home," I heard Red say.

"And they're not at the river," Shaggy said.

"Met Somov. Alone," Val reported to Iron Button. "Asked where Bessoltseva was. He said he didn't know. I think he was lying."

"You're all so useless," Iron Button shouted angrily. "You can't do the simplest task—finding one stupid girl."

They all fell silent.

"And here comes Vasiliev, the bleeding heart," Iron Button said disdainfully. When he got close, Shaggy shoved him.

"What's the matter with you?" Vasiliev said. "Are you crazy?"

"You're a turncoat," Iron Button said.

"A turncoat?" Vasiliev said. "Where did I turn to?"

"You let them go, didn't you?" Val shouted.

"Shaggy, you're breaking my arm." I could hear the pain in Vasiliev's voice. "I'm also against treachery!" he said. "We didn't give her a chance, she's a girl!"

"So what!" Red was angry. "She snitched, so she has to pay the consequences."

"Red, you're damn right," Shaggy agreed.

"You bet I am!" Red said with a tinge of sadness in his voice. "I was expected in Moscow. I won't forgive her for this."

"He was expected in Moscow! A prince! They were preparing a parade with flags and balloons and a three-course banquet for him," Val clowned. "Who would be expecting you in Moscow, you pathetic red-haired creep—"

"I *was* expected!" Red said, then added softly, "My father was waiting for me."

"Your father!" Val choked with laughter. "If you have a father, then why do you have your mother's name? Hah!" He shouted in Red's face, "Bastard!"

Red hung his head low and didn't say anything.

"Oh, shut up!" Shaggy said to Val.

"Why is he lying?" Val yelled. "Everyone knows he doesn't have a father."

"I told you to shut up," Shaggy said threateningly.

Then I heard Popov's voice. "Hey, gang!" he cried excitedly. "Somov's father has a new car."

"Where's Bessoltseva?" Iron Button demanded.

"I don't know. But it's the latest model car."

"Who cares!" Iron Button said. "We have to deal with Somov first."

"What about?" Shmakova wanted to know.

"Somov has to agree to stop protecting Bessoltseva. If he doesn't . . ."

It was at this point that I opened the door and floated out. I felt beautiful. Instead of braids, I had long, silky curls cascading down to my shoulders.

They couldn't believe their eyes. They stared at me.

"That's really cool!" Shmakova said enviously.

But Val stepped forward and hissed, "Surround her."

The gang moved in on me slowly. They knew I had nowhere to run and they took their time. Only Vasiliev stood to the side.

I recoiled in fright. My eyes darted this way

and that. Where was Dimka? He had promised to wait for me.

"Who's that gorgeous blonde?" Val wanted to know.

Red shaded his eyes and said, "Where? Where?"

"She doesn't even notice us!" Shaggy cried in mock anger. "She's so stuck up!"

"Lena, it's us, your classmates," Shmakova sang.

"We'll get her attention! It'll hurt, but . . ." Val took out a peashooter, aimed, and fired.

I touched my cheek. It felt like a bee sting.

"She's noticed us!" Shaggy smirked.

I wanted to cry out in pain and humiliation, but instead I stood there like a marionette on a string, jerkily clutching various parts of my body as Val kept shooting at me, calmly, deliberately—my nose, my cheek, my lips!

Just then the beauty-parlor door opened and Mrs. Klava stood in the doorway. A pea hit her in the arm. Her face got angry.

"You hooligan!" she screamed at Val. "How dare you!"

"Mrs. Klava, I wasn't aiming at you, I was aiming at her!" Val pointed at me. "She's a snake."

"What's going on here?" Mrs. Klava wanted to know.

"She's a bitch, and you did her hair!" shouted Red, trying to hit me.

"What's the matter with you? Tolya!" Mrs. Klava grabbed her son's hand.

"Leave me alone!" screamed Red, and pulled away from his mother.

"We're just playing, Mrs. Klava," Val explained.

Val and Shaggy grabbed me and started pulling me away. I resisted. I was afraid to leave Mrs. Klava.

"Carry her!" Iron Button commanded.

"Carry her like a princess! She's our maiden!" Shmakova laughed. "Big Mouth!" Then she called to Popov, "Why are you just standing there? Do something!"

Popov ran to help Shaggy and Val. The three of them tried to pick me up and drag me away.

"Dimka!" I shrieked desperately.

"Leave her alone!" Mrs. Klava tried to push them aside. "This is ridiculous! You'll ruin her hair!"

Vasiliev rushed to help Mrs. Klava, shouting, "You can't hit girls!" He pushed me past Shmakova, who tried to block my path.

"Tolya!" Mrs. Klava cried. "Come back! Tolya!"

But Tolya ignored her.

Mrs. Klava shook her head sadly. "What a

shame they didn't go to Moscow. Go try to understand them. Who's right, who's wrong?" She looked at Vasiliev. "Do you know why they're after her?"

"No," Vasiliev said grimly.

"I thought so. None of you ever knows anything." Mrs. Klava went back into the beauty parlor.

Then everything happened at once. Shaggy knocked down Vasiliev. Mironova rushed at me. The others followed Iron Button, hooting and whistling.

7

Can you imagine, Grandfather? They chased me through town in broad daylight. Have you ever been chased like a hare? You can't run. If you run, that means you're guilty, so you have to stand your ground and fight back, even if you're outnumbered. I didn't know that and I ran.

They chased me, shouting, "Scarecrow! Snitch! Traitor!"

Passersby stared at me. I would slow down so it would look like I wasn't running, like it wasn't me they were chasing.

Once they caught up with me, and Val grabbed my arm. But I pulled away and managed to reach our street. The whole gang came after me!

I ran inside the house, but you weren't home. I wondered what had happened to Dimka. So I went outside and peeked through the crack in the gates. And there was the gang, with Dimka in the middle. He was waving his arms and talking; it looked like he was trying to convince them of something. *Good,* I thought, *he's finally telling them the truth.* I felt happy: They must be so ashamed of treating a human being like a hare!

I waited and waited, but no one came. When it got dark, I went back inside and waited there. I couldn't wait anymore, I just couldn't take it—do you understand, Grandfather?—so I phoned Dimka. His sister answered. "Dimka isn't home," she said. "Your boyfriend's out."

I laughed. "I had my hair done," I said. "Mrs. Klava says I'm beautiful now." I hung up. Then I jumped around the house, dancing and repeating, "Your boyfriend. Your boyfriend."

Just then someone knocked at the window.

"Dimka!" I shouted, and hurried to open the window.

A huge bear face loomed in. It looked like a bear. A real bear! And it growled, "ROAR!"

I was so frightened I jumped away from the window and put out the light, so I wouldn't be seen from the street. I pressed myself against the wall and stood there trembling. Then I heard the door slam, and I shouted, "Who's there?" and it was you, Grandfather, remember?

Nikolai Nikolayevich nodded. He remembered that day very well—it was the day

Grandma Kolkina gave him *Mashka.* And she wouldn't take any money from him. She *gave* him *Mashka.* He was as happy as a child as he hurried home—he wanted to show the portrait to Lena and hang it on the wall where it belonged.

He remembered hearing Lena's desperate voice crying, "Who's there?" as he entered the house.

Not realizing that something was wrong, he said joyously, "Look what I've brought!"

Then he saw Lena's frightened face. He did not understand what was happening to the person he loved more than anyone, his granddaughter, his own flesh and blood.

"Outside the window," Lena whispered, "there's a bear."

"A bear? Polar or grizzly?" he joked.

"I'm telling you, someone is out there wearing a bear head. He tried to get inside."

Nikolai Nikolayevich went over to the window and looked out. "There's no one there," he said. "It must be your imagination." And he started to unwrap Mashka's portrait. "Just look at it, Lena!" he said happily. "Grandma Kolkina gave it to us as a gift. I wanted to pay, but she wouldn't take any money."

He put the portrait in front of Lena, watching her face. "How do you like her? Isn't she wonderful?"

"She sort of looks like me," Lena said.

Nikolai Nikolayevich looked at the painting, then at Lena—there definitely was a resemblance. "Lena!" he shouted happily. "You're her double! Look! The same color eyes, the mouth . . ."

"A big mouth," Lena said sadly. "Maybe that's what they called her, too?"

Only then did he notice Lena's hair. "Where are your braids?"

"I had my hair done, just for the vacation," she said, and smiled shyly, the corners of her mouth stretching toward her ears.

Nikolai Nikolayevich turned the painting over and looked at the date: 1870. "She," he said, pointing to *Mashka,* "gave this painting to one of her favorite students. She's my grandfather's sister. I remember her well. She used to live in your room. When she died, the whole town came to her funeral."

Nikolai Nikolayevich ran around the room, rubbing his hands, panting, clutching his heart. "My God!" he exclaimed. "You look so much like her! My work is coming to an end. I've collected almost all the portraits. Now I can invite someone from the museum to come and view our treasures. They'll ooh and aah and say, 'You've discovered a new, little-known artist.' And we'll spend long winter evenings making plans."

"What kind of plans?" Lena asked.

"Big plans." Nikolai Nikolayevich smiled, not noticing the note of sadness in Lena's voice. "We have a lot to decide on."

Just then the growling bear head appeared in the window again.

"The bear!" screamed Lena, and jumped up on a chair.

Nikolai Nikolayevich rushed over to the window, grabbed the bear head, and threw it on the couch—exposing Dimka! A frightened, pathetic Dimka.

Something strange was going on. He sensed that something had gone wrong. He looked at Lena. She stood there motionless for a second, then the next moment she was at the window, shouting, "Dimka! Dimka-a-a-a!"

But Dimka was gone.

In despair she turned to Nikolai Nikolayevich. "Grandfather! They made him scare me, I know it, Grandfather. Do something! Shout at them, scare them!"

Nikolai Nikolayevich saw a small band of kids standing not far from the house in a pool of weak electric light, and among them was Dimka, trying to hide behind their backs.

"Dimka-a-a!" Lena called again.

"Maybe he's not there," Nikolai Nikolayevich

said, hoping Lena didn't notice him.

"I see him, Grandfather! Shout at them! Save him!"

Nikolai Nikolayevich filled his lungs with air. "Let go of Dimka right now!"

Laughter was the response.

Lena grabbed her jacket and rushed to the door. Nikolai Nikolayevich tried to stop her. "Let go of me!" Lena shouted, gasping for breath. "He could choke to death if they stick a gag in his mouth! I have to help him!" She twisted out of his grasp and ran.

"Lena-a-a-a!" Nikolai Nikolayevich called, without any hope of getting an answer.

Nikolai Nikolayevich was about to go out after her, when his eye fell on *Mashka*. Mashka's almost transparent figure seemed to float in the air.

He was transfixed. Mesmerized.

He heard the shattering of glass somewhere. Someone shouting, "There she is! Get her!" But his mind was lost in the painting, as if in a trance. Nikolai Nikolayevich took out his old notebook and started to write. Lena and her troubles were somewhere far, far in the distance.

He could faintly hear voices under his window: "She's not in the room."

"Patches is scratching away at his desk—what a scene!"

"What if she didn't throw the rock?"

"I saw her, I did."

"She's jealous of you."

"She broke the window."

But Nikolai Nikolayevich was totally oblivious. He leafed through his notebook, writing down his thoughts and guesses about the various family portraits.

It was only when Lena came back, her dress and jacket covered with mud, her eyes shut as she leaned strangely against the door and slowly slid down to the floor, that Nikolai Nikolayevich came to. He rushed over to help her up. He led her to the couch and covered her with a blanket.

"What is the matter, child?" Nikolai Nikolayevich kneeled by the couch. "Lena!" Lena lay there, deathly white. Nikolai Nikolayevich did not hope for an answer, but suddenly Lena said in a loud, piteous, sobbing voice, "Grandfather, he tricked me!"

"Tricked you?"

"Yes! There he was with Mironova and the rest of them in his house. They were all there, Grandfather! They were watching TV and drinking tea," she said, sobbing even louder. "I thought he was tied up and gagged, and I wanted to help him. But he was there with them . . . having tea."

"So what?" Nikolai Nikolayevich tried to console her. "Why don't we have some tea too?"

"How can you talk about tea, Grandfather! I have to tell you what I did. I picked up a rock and threw it at them through the window." Lena burst into tears.

"I think I heard that. . . . Go ahead and have a good cry. You'll feel better."

Nikolai Nikolayevich didn't know what to say or do. Lena's eyes were shut. He got up and stood in the middle of the room for a while, then he picked up the bear head and put it on the table. He sat in his father's chair and mechanically opened his book and started on his notations again: *A painting by the artist Nikolai Nikolayevich I. Bessoltsev, depicting his daughter Mashka at the age of eleven or twelve. This is the artist's last work, done shortly before his death.*

8

The day after, while I was washing my dress, I kept thinking about Dimka. And then I realized something: I hated him!

Blood rushed to my head, I ran into my room and began packing. *I'll show him! He'll write me letters and I won't answer!* I thought. *Ten a day, a hundred a day, I won't answer! Never!*

I was running around the room grabbing things and stuffing them in my bag when I saw Dimka in our yard.

I grabbed the dress I was ironing and ran out to hang it on the line. My heart was leaping!

I pretended that I didn't know he was behind me, breathing down my neck. At last I turned around. He was standing there with his head bowed. "I guess you don't even want to know who I am," he said.

I tried to be calm and, more important, unapproachable. So when he said that, I smiled slightly. "I know who you are, you are Dimka Somov," I said slowly, so he wouldn't hear my voice trembling; then I looked at him and saw that he was more nervous than me!

"If you knew who I really was, you wouldn't smile or joke." He stopped for a second, then whispered, "I'm a louse! The lowest of the low, a coward!"

When he said that, his face got all blotchy, with bright-red spots, as if someone had used red paint on him.

"You're no coward," I said reassuringly. "You saved dogs from Val! You weren't afraid of Pete! You told Margarita Ivanovna the truth!"

"No, no, no! Margarita Ivanovna was right; I'm a pathetic coward! Do you know why I told her the truth? Because I wanted to prove to myself that I wasn't afraid of anything. But I am, I can't bring myself to tell the gang that it was I who snitched. I thought I'd tell them at the movies and prove to myself that I'm not a coward. But when I saw them, I got scared. I wanted to tell them in the morning at school, in front of the whole class and Margarita Ivanovna. But there was the principal's note, and I chickened out again. Then I waited for Margarita Ivanovna to leave, I was planning to do it then, but I couldn't. And then, when Iron Button declared the boycott against you, I got so scared.

And that evening I had gone to the gang meaning to tell them everything, and they talked me into putting on the bear head, and . . . I know I'm a nothing, I'm a louse." He raised his eyes and I saw that they were filled with tears.

"But I promise you, on my honor, I will tell them the truth. Now! Will you come with me?"

And I believed him. "Of course I'll come," I said, and blushed. I'm so stupid.

And Dimka put his arm around me and kissed me! Can you believe that, Grandfather, he kissed me! I laughed at first, but then I just stood there. I might have stood that way till morning if Val hadn't shown up.

"Gotcha, Somov!" he shouted. "You're through now! Time for the funeral march . . . dum-de-dum-dum . . ." He laughed. "I'll tell the gang about you and Bessoltseva!" He pulled my dress off the line. I tried to get it back, but he jumped away. "So long, Scarecrow!" He waved my dress over his head. "Bring the bear head and you can have your dress!"

"You're a creep. Give back that dress!" Dimka shouted.

"You're going to dance to my tune now!" Val yelled back. "I'll tell the gang you're sweet on Scarecrow!" He laughed again and ran off.

"Don't worry!" Dimka said to me. "I'll get your dress back. Soon. Today. Right now! And

I'll tell them everything!"

"Wait," I said.

I ran back into the house and brought him the bear head. "I'll go with you!"

"No, I'll do it myself," he said resolutely. "Wait for me." And he waved the bear head at me in farewell.

I thought I had made a mistake letting Dimka go off on his own, so I ran after him.

I didn't catch up with him; he ducked into a shed where Iron Button's gang was waiting. I found a hole in the rotten wall and looked through it, thinking that if Dimka needed me I would be right there.

They were all there, rolling on the floor, laughing at Red, who was wearing my dress. Red was imitating me: tripping over his own feet, falling, turning his head, smiling from ear to ear. They were having a great time. Only Mironova sat apart.

"He really is a good actor," Lena said sadly. "He kind of looked like me. . . ."

"What was Dimka doing?" Nikolai Nikolaye-vich wanted to know.

"Dimka?"

Dimka came up to Val and threw the bear head at him. "Take it," he said, his voice cracking. "And you, Red, take off the dress."

Dimka began pulling the dress off Red. "Don't touch me! I'm ticklish!" shouted Red, pushing Dimka away.

They all laughed again at Red's imitation of me.

Iron Button, without moving or turning her head in Dimka's direction, said, "Somov, why don't you tell us where you just came from?"

Dimka pretended not to hear her. He was clutching my dress the way a drowning man might clutch at straws. "Quit fooling around — you're going to rip the dress," he said, and pulled hard on Red.

"Red, kick him!" Val shouted.

Red obeyed. Then Shaggy came up from behind, and he and Red twisted Dimka's arms behind him.

Val exulted. "Why don't you tell Mironova where you were? Huh? Tell Iron Button where you were, Dimka boy. No? Then I'll tell them. This is big news, gang! Dimka was with Scarecrow!" He screeched and spun around on one foot. "Do you know what they were doing? Kissing!"

"Kissing?" Shmakova asked. "Bessoltseva? You're making it up!"

"Smack on the lips! Working for both sides, are you, Somov?"

"Shut up!" Dimka tried to get out of Shaggy's grasp.

Val took advantage and hit Dimka. "Traitor!" he screamed, and hit him again.

Dimka was incensed. "You lousy skinner! Do you guys know what our Val does?"

"Shut up, creep!" Val yelled, and hit him again.

Dimka was furious. He pushed Shaggy and Red aside and hit Val so hard he flew across the shed and fell at the feet of the unperturbed Iron Button.

When Val saw that Dimka wasn't pursuing him, he spat, "You better watch it, Somov—there's a lot of us and you're alone. We'll make you into hamburger."

"Right, hamburger!" said Shaggy, taking a step toward Dimka.

"Hamburger!" said Red.

Then Popov joined them—Shmakova told him to.

Can you imagine, four against one?

I was going to rush in and help when Dimka grabbed a long pole and waved it around. "Come on, come! I'm waiting! Just try it!"

"You know, Grandfather, I was so proud of him. Dimka didn't need my help. If you could have seen their faces! They were afraid!"

Lena's laughter pealed and her face bloomed

suddenly, eyes sparkling. Nikolai Nikolayevich looked at Lena and smiled—she was so lovely, and so trusting, and she was his dear, beloved granddaughter.

Dimka moved forward with the pole in front of him, and they backed off.

Suddenly Iron Button blocked his path. "Give me the stick!" she ordered.

Dimka threw the stick at Iron Button's feet. "Some heroes," he said scornfully. "Hiding behind a girl!"

Val grabbed it just in case.

"What were you doing at her house?" Mironova asked.

"That's my business," Dimka replied.

"Mr. Courage!" Val interjected. He was playing with the stick and circling behind Dimka.

"Did you feel sorry for her?" Mironova continued her interrogation.

"Let's say I did."

"You sap!" She said it harshly and turned away from him in disgust.

Dimka mustered his courage and said, "Well, what if she didn't snitch?"

"You're just putty and mush!" Mironova snapped like the crack of a whip.

Dimka's voice broke completely. "Well, and what if I was the one who did it?" And he smiled challengingly at them all.

"You?" She gave Dimka a hard look. "Now that's an interesting possibility!"

"What if it's true?" Vasiliev said.

And Shmakova sang, "It's quite possible."

"And how!" Popov exclaimed.

"Then I would feel sorry for you," Shaggy said.

"And that fool Bessoltseva was covering for you." Iron Button figured it out.

There was a silence. Everyone stared at Dimka.

He smiled crookedly, his eyes darting with fear. "A guy can't even make a joke," he said. "No one has a sense of humor around here."

Mironova didn't really understand jokes. "Look me in the eye," she said. "In the eye!" she shouted.

Dimka pushed her aside. He didn't want to look into her eyes. "Leave me alone. I told you, it's a joke!" He laughed unnaturally. "A joke!" He winked.

But they didn't believe Dimka—they all attacked him. They had him up against the wall—I couldn't see him, but I could hear him crying out, "You're crazy! . . . I wanted to help—Bessoltseva—I felt sorry for her—"

I rushed into the shed and bit and scratched my way to him, shouting, "Leave him alone! Leave him alone!"

"Look, it's Scarecrow!" Vasiliev whispered in disbelief.

"Did you come to help your boyfriend?" Red shouted.

"Yes."

"And you're not afraid?" Shaggy asked.

"No." I turned to Dimka and smiled—it was pathetic, but it was a smile. "I got tired of waiting, so I came."

Dimka said nothing.

Val laughed. "I think they're exchanging vows."

"Wait, Val," Iron Button said. "Bessoltseva, why did you come?"

I didn't want to say anything, I wanted Dimka to speak. But Dimka said nothing.

"Let's have a confrontation," Shmakova said sweetly. "It's so interesting."

"Bessoltseva," Iron Button said, "which one of you is the traitor?" She looked first at me, then at Dimka, then at me again. "You or Somov?"

I looked at Dimka and said, "Me, of course."

"Just as I thought," Iron Button said. "Somov felt sorry for her. I told you he was a sap." She turned to me and her face blazed with righteous indignation. "Well, why are you silent? Maybe we'll forgive you. Maybe you'll make us feel sorry for you."

I waited for her to finish and said to Red,

"Take off my dress."

"All right," Red said. He took it off and held it out for me. "Here. . . ." And he threw it over my head to Shaggy. Shaggy shook the dress under my nose and tossed it to Val. . . . And so it went. Val to Shmakova, Shmakova to Popov, Popov to someone else. Faster, faster!

The circle of faces swam before my eyes, and I ran in circles like a hamster in a wheel.

I should have left, forgetting about the dress and about the gang, but I was so stupid, I kept trying, trying to win. Not for my sake, for Dimka's sake.

And suddenly someone threw the dress to Dimka. And he caught it. I felt the tense silence.

Mironova said, "Here's your confrontation, Shmakova. Now we'll learn the real truth!"

I went over to Dimka, reached for the dress, and smiled. "Let's go!" I said.

He did not budge and did not give me my dress, but he smiled back. So I smiled again, my hand was still out for the dress.

And then . . . Dimka threw the dress over my head to Mironova!

"Good for you, Somov!" Iron Button congratulated him.

And I—I slapped Dimka's face!

Lena looked at her hand, her body quivering with great pain somewhere deep inside.

Nikolai Nikolayevich felt a great pain also. He too had slapped a face. And whose? Lena's! For what? For threatening to sell a painting.

"Forgive me, Lena." Nikolai Nikolayevich touched her cheek. "I've never hit anyone in my life." He looked at the portraits on the walls. "And all because of those."

"I've already forgiven you," Lena said, and hugged Nikolai Nikolayevich. "Now listen to what happened next."

"Burn her at the stake!" Red shouted.

"Drag her into the garden," cried Iron Button.

I fought and kicked as hard as I could, but they got me out into the garden.

Iron Button and Shaggy brought out a scarecrow on a long stick. Dimka followed them. They dressed the scarecrow in my dress, and painted my eyes and my big mouth on its head. The legs were made of stockings stuffed with straw, and there was a mop for hair and some feathers. Around the dummy's neck was a sign:

SCARECROW
IS A
TRAITOR

Lena stopped talking and seemed to fade somehow.

Nikolai Nikolayevich realized she was coming

to the end of her story and the end of her strength.

They gathered around the scarecrow. Jumping and laughing, shouting, "Here she is, our beauty! Our maiden in distress!"

"Let Dimka light the bonfire!" sang Shmakova.

And I thought, *If Dimka lights the fire, I'll just die.*

Val had already stuck the pole in the ground and was piling kindling under it.

"I don't have any matches," Dimka said softly.

"But I do!" Shaggy shoved a matchbox in Dimka's hands and shoved him forward.

Dimka stood by the dummy, his head hanging low.

He's going to confess now, I thought. *He'll look around and say, "Gang, Lena isn't guilty of anything. I did it!"* But he just stood there.

"Light it!" ordered Iron Button.

I couldn't stand it. "Dimka! Don't do it, Dimka!" I begged.

He looked so small and fragile, almost insignificant.

"Well, Somov!" said Iron Button.

And you know what Dimka did, Grandfather?

Dimka fell to his knees and struck the match. The flames rose up and over his shoulders.

They dragged me to the fire. I didn't struggle;

I watched the flames. Grandfather, I could feel the heat of the fire engulf me, burning and biting me.

I screamed. I screamed so loud that they let go of me.

I reached into the fire, scattering it with my feet, picking up hot branches with my hands — I didn't want the effigy to burn: I desperately wanted to save it.

Dimka was the first to come to his senses. "Are you nuts?" He grabbed me by the arm and tried to pull me away.

I pushed him off so hard he fell over backward. I pulled the effigy from the fire and waved it over my head, attacking them. The scarecrow had already caught fire, and sparks showered from it in all directions.

"If you burn my jacket," Shmakova squealed, "you'll pay for it!"

"She's crazy!" Red shouted.

They all scattered.

I got so dizzy chasing after them I couldn't stop until I fell. The effigy lay on the ground next to me. It was scorched but it seemed alive.

I just lay there with my eyes shut. Then I smelled something burning and opened my eyes — the scarecrow's dress was smoking. I stamped the burning hem with my hand and fell back in the grass.

I heard Iron Button's voice asking, "Why did you stop? Feeling sorry for her again?"

I looked up and saw Mironova and Dimka.

I felt as if I were in a deep, deep well, and Mironova's voice, echoing from somewhere high above me, hurt my ears.

"You're a weakling, Somov! She's a traitor, you have to remember that."

I heard branches snap, receding footsteps, and then silence.

I don't know how long I lay there — maybe an hour, maybe a minute — until I felt someone watching me. I looked around and saw Dimka hiding in the bushes. He pushed the branches aside and slowly came over to me.

"You know, Grandfather," Lena said in a sad voice, "it was then that I realized my life was over."

"What nonsense, child!" Nikolai Nikolayevich whispered. "What did Dimka say?"

He said that he had tried to tell them the truth but they wouldn't believe him. He said he wouldn't give up trying to convince them it was he who was guilty.

I think I said something to him, but maybe I didn't. I don't remember.

He talked on and on about "believing and

108

not believing," about how they'd understand.
I listened and I smiled—out of embarrassment
and shame for him. But when he saw me smile,
he thought I had forgiven him, and his voice
grew stronger and rang out, flying up with the
sparks of the dying bonfire, the very fire he
had just lit to betray and humiliate me.

I began taking my dress off the effigy. It was
burned in several places. I burned myself and
cried out in pain. Dimka reached out to touch
my cheek. "You're bleeding."

I jumped back as if burned. "Don't touch
me! Don't you dare touch me!" I screamed at
him.

"Grandfather, I thought, I felt, that if he
touched me it would hurt like fire. I couldn't
stand him anymore; I didn't want to see him
anymore. I ran to the river and hid under an
old overturned boat for a long time."

"I was frantic, child," said Nikolai Nikolayevich. "I ran everywhere looking for you."

"I heard you calling me, but I couldn't come
out. I might never have come out, if this little
dog hadn't climbed under the boat. It was so
pathetic, worse than me. It began licking my
hands, and I saw that it was hungry. So I got
out, brought it out, and fed it."

Vacation was over and we had to go back to school. When I found out that Margarita Ivanovna wasn't back, I spent the day at the wharf, watching the river and waiting for her. When I saw her, I rushed to her like a crazy person, but she didn't even notice me as she and her new husband got off the boat. I watched them go past me, up the steps of the cliff, gazing at each other and not seeing anything around them. I raced ahead and slowly walked back toward them. They walked right past me again. He was holding her elbow and whispering in her ear. She was listening intently and smiling.

The following morning I did go to school. I came in after the bell, behind Margarita Ivanovna.

When I appeared in the doorway of the classroom, all heads turned in my direction, like windup dolls. I looked at Dimka's scared face,

Shmakova's sly, foxy one, and Iron Button's stern one, then I stared at Margarita Ivanovna.

"Hello, Margarita Ivanovna," I said.

I was waiting for her to ask me about the boycott. But all Margarita Ivanovna said was, "Hello, hello, Bessoltseva. Why are you staring? Come in, come in." She bent over the roll book.

I walked right up to the desk, waiting for her to look at me and ask me about the boycott. Finally she looked up and said, "Do you want to tell me something?" Without waiting for an answer, she got up, went over to the window, and waved.

"The husband, the husband, the husband," the class whispered.

"Margarita Ivanovna," Shmakova sang, "is that your husband sitting on the bench?"

"Yes, it is," Margarita Ivanovna said.

"Will you introduce us to him?"

"I will." Margarita Ivanovna tried to contain a smile.

I kept staring at her, staring. . . .

"And now," she said, "let's get to work." She noticed my stare. "Why are you staring, Bessoltseva? Have I changed?"

"No, I'm just glad you're back."

She was beginning to look impatient.

"When you were leaving, you said, 'Wait till I get back!' " I practically shouted at her.

"I was angry with you then," Margarita Ivanovna said.

I nodded happily: *Now she'll ask me.*

"But"—Margarita Ivanovna waved her hand merrily—"you've been punished enough. There's no point in dwelling in the past." She laughed. "Sit down, Bessoltseva, and we'll start class."

"I won't sit down!" I shouted. "I'm leaving forever. I just came to say good-bye." And I ran out of the classroom.

"Bessoltseva, wait!" Margarita Ivanovna called after me.

But I didn't wait. Why should I wait! They didn't want to know the truth! They didn't want to know that Dimka had sold me out a hundred times over. Grandfather! I thought Margarita Ivanovna would make everything right. But she came back and didn't remember a thing.

"They're the ones who will be sorry," Nikolai Nikolayevich said.

"Not Iron Button and her friends," Lena said. Suddenly tears filled her eyes. "Listen, Grandfather!" she whispered. "I'm no better than Dimka. Don't smile! I betrayed you! I was ashamed of you—I was ashamed that you went around in patches and old galoshes. You are my grandfather! Dimka once asked me why you went

112

around looking like a beggar. He said everyone laughs at you and calls you Patches."

Lena stopped.

"Do you think I defended you? No, Grandfather, I didn't! Instead, I started feeling ashamed of you. Whenever I would see you in the street, I would hide and wait for you to go around the corner. And sometimes you would walk so slowly, the taps on your shoes would go *click-click*, and you looked so lonely, as if everyone in the world had abandoned you."

"You have an overactive imagination, child." Nikolai Nikolayevich quickly bent over and retied his shoelace.

"Grandfather! Did you ever notice me hiding from you?"

"No," Nikolai Nikolayevich said firmly, "not even once."

"You did, I know you did! How could I have been ashamed of you? I'm no good, I'm no good, Grandfather."

"You didn't hurt my feelings. Well, maybe just a little," Nikolai Nikolayevich admitted. "I knew you'd understand me in time. It didn't matter when.

"I had an old army friend and he didn't understand me at first either. He came to visit me, and when he saw my coat, he started yelling at me. 'How could you have sunk so low? You have a good pension from the army. You should be like me.' He was so neat and clean, dressed perfectly. Tailored clothes . . .

"While he was here, two people from the regional museum came to see me, trying to get me to sell the portrait of General Rayevsky. They offered me two thousand rubles. But I refused, of course.

"My friend reprimanded me and kept suggesting things I could do with the money.

"I told him I didn't have the right to sell the portrait—it belonged not to me alone but to our whole family: my son, you, your future family!

"My friend was so embarrassed, he left almost immediately, slamming the door. An hour later he was back with a package. He said, 'Don't be insulted, my friend. Members of the regiment can help each other out.'

"It was a new coat. I tried it on, praised it, thanked him. After he left, I took it back to the store and sent him the money. I figured he'd reprimand me for that too. But he understood, and apologized."

"Grandfather, please don't think I don't like your portraits," Lena said unexpectedly. "I love them. It will be hard for me to leave them."

"Oh, my dear child," said Nikolai Nikolayevich happily. "You're definitely a Bessoltsev."

114

"Others like your paintings too," Lena said, smiling at him. "Honest."

"Who, for instance?" asked Nikolai Nikolayevich.

"Vasiliev. He came over once. 'This is like a museum,' he said. 'Too bad no one ever sees them.'"

For some reason Lena's words made Nikolai Nikolayevich uneasy. He walked over to General Rayevsky's portrait and stared at it for a long time. "Your Vasiliev was right," he finally said. "You can't even imagine how right he was!"

It got dark outside, but neither Lena nor Nikolai Nikolayevich bothered to turn on the lights.

Lena continued her packing, moving around the room putting things in a suitcase. She had to get out of here. They were all foxes, wolves, jackals! It was so hard to wait until tomorrow! The music next door continued. Lena heard excited voices as Dimka's guests came outside. She heard shouts of pleasure — Dimka's father was driving them home in his new car, and Dimka was giving orders, who would sit in front, who in back.

They were happy, they were together, and she was alone — a mouse in a mousetrap.

Maybe she should go over and tell them it was Dimka who snitched, and then he would be alone and she would be one of them?

115

But something wouldn't let her do it. What was it, pride? Anger with Dimka?

She was throwing one thing after another into the suitcase when she heard someone say, "Hello!"

Nikolai Nikolayevich switched on the light — it was Vasiliev.

"Grandfather, this is Vasiliev," said Lena.

"Hello," Vasiliev said again. "Your door was open. . . ."

"Come in, come in," Nikolai Nikolayevich said pleasantly. "We were just talking about you. Lena said that you like our portraits." Nikolai Nikolayevich clutched at Vasiliev. He had come over. That meant he liked Lena, didn't it?

"I like them," Vasiliev said, glancing at the suitcase.

"Which one do you like best?" Nikolai Nikolayevich insisted.

"That one." Vasiliev pointed at General Rayevsky. "Who is he?" he asked mechanically.

Nikolai Nikolayevich spoke gladly. "Why, he's a hero of the Napoleonic War of 1812, General Rayevsky. My great-grandfather painted his portrait. He was a famous man."

Vasiliev looked at Lena and suddenly asked, "So you're leaving? Then you really are guilty."

"That's not true!" Nikolai Nikolayevich was outraged. "Lena's not guilty of anything!"

"Then why is she leaving?" Vasiliev wanted to know.

"It's none of your business!" Lena replied.

"Coward!" Vasiliev said. "You're running away!"

"I'm not afraid of anything!" Lena cried out. "Grandfather, tell him I'm not afraid of anything. Anything. I'll prove it to everyone!" She ran out of the room and minutes later was back, wearing the dress that had burned on the effigy. "I'll show everyone that I'm not afraid," she said softly, and ran out of the room.

Vasiliev started after her, but Nikolai Nikolayevich stopped him. "She knows what she's doing," he said.

"But why does she want to leave?" Vasiliev demanded stubbornly.

Nikolai Nikolayevich looked at Vasiliev — at his thin face, his glasses with only one lens, his tight lips, his virtuous manner — and for some reason lost his temper. "Leave, Vasiliev! I've gotten rather sick of you!" He pushed him out the door.

Then Nikolai Nikolayevich climbed the stairs and went out on the balcony facing Dimka's house. He peered into the dark and saw Lena's figure flash between the dark tree trunks, cross the street, and vanish around the corner.

Where's she going? Nikolai Nikolayevich

117

thought worriedly. Trying to calm himself, he began thinking about the family portraits that surrounded him; then he thought about his long-dead relatives, his brothers and sisters. Nikolai Nikolayevich could almost feel the warmth of their hands, could hear their laughter and arguments. They were with him! He was glad Lena resembled Mashka. It was a link to the past. Lena! His beloved Lena. His granddaughter. And suddenly Nikolai Nikolayevich felt a great strength in his body and he laughed. He knew what he had to do.

10

Lena was in a hurry; she had to get to the beauty parlor before it closed. She tore into the parlor barely able to breathe.

Mrs. Klava was sitting alone, reading. She raised her tired eyes to Lena and said with hostility, "Look who's here," and turned away.

"Hello, Mrs. Klava."

Mrs. Klava looked at her watch, got up, and started putting away her scissors, combs, and dryer. "Want to have you hair done again, huh? You liked it. . . . Well, I won't do it," she said.

"You don't want to cut my hair?" Lena asked.

"I don't," Mrs. Klava said. "The work day is over."

"Why? You think I'm a traitor?"

"I don't have the right to select my clients," said Mrs. Klava. "I have to service people whether I like them or not." Suddenly she said in a trembling voice, "My boy's father lives in

119

Moscow. He hasn't seen him in three long years. Tolya couldn't sleep nights, thinking about seeing his father again—what they would talk about, where they would go. And you chopped my Red right off at the ankles!"

"It wasn't me," Lena said without thinking. "I wasn't the one who snitched."

"Why are you lying?" Mrs. Klava asked. Lena could see she was upset. "Over some stupid hairdo. You really are a baby!"

"I'm not lying. Honest! I took the blame for someone else."

"What did you do that for?" Mrs. Klava squinted at her suspiciously.

"I wanted to help someone," Lena said.

"And what did he do?" Mrs. Klava asked.

"Nothing. He said he'd admit his guilt later."

"And what did you do?"

"I'm still keeping quiet."

"But why?" Mrs. Klava was visibly taken back. "Maybe you should tell the kids the truth? They'll understand. . . ." But she saw that Lena wasn't listening, and she stopped. "Well, I'm not going to tell you what to do, you have to decide yourself. Just don't let whoever it is get away with it."

Lena said nothing.

"Oh, well," Mrs. Klava said, "I guess you've decided to let him get away with it."

"No, I haven't," Lena said.

"Sit down, then. I'll make you so beautiful he'll confess to things he didn't do."

Mrs. Klava started to untie the ribbons in Lena's braids.

"Don't bother undoing the braids. I want you to shave my head."

"Have you gone nuts? I won't do that!"

"They call me Scarecrow!" Lena said.

"So what? They call my boy Red," said Mrs. Klava.

"I want them to see how ugly I am, that I'm a real scarecrow."

"Don't talk nonsense, girl! Why don't I give you a gorgeous hairdo instead." Mrs. Klava smiled and began combing out Lena's hair. "You'll see! When you see yourself in the mirror, you'll change your mind."

Lena jumped out of the chair. "I'm a scarecrow! Do you understand? I'll show them how ugly a scarecrow can be!" She grabbed the scissors and started chopping at her hair.

"Are you crazy?" Mrs. Klava rushed toward her, trying to grab away the scissors. "Stop it!"

Lena ran around the room, cutting her hair and shouting, "I'm a scarecrow! I'm a scarecrow!"

By the time Mrs. Klava managed to catch her, Lena had hacked off huge chunks of her hair.

"What have you done?" Mrs. Klava wailed,

holding Lena and rocking her like a small child. "You poor thing. My Tolya was so mad at you. He wanted to see his father so desperately he cried, he cried like a baby."

"I didn't know, Mrs. Klava, truly I didn't. I'm so sorry."

"Sit down, girl. I'll cut your hair any way you want."

Lena sat down, and Mrs. Klava covered her with a sheet.

The party at Dimka Somov's was coming to an end. Most of the kids had left, and only Mironova's gang remained.

"Let's party till dawn!" Shmakova sang.

"Good thinking, Shmakova!" Popov cried.

Shmakova's ideas were always good as far as Popov was concerned.

"Shaggy, you can sleep over at my house," Red said.

"Thanks, Red. You're a real pal."

Val turned on the stereo full blast. "Let's rattle the Bessoltsevs' windows!" He laughed. "We're having a great time!"

Shmakova took Dimka's hand and they danced. Shmakova spun and twisted—she was in her element.

Suddenly the door opened and Lena burst into the room.

Her knit cap was pulled low over her brow, her jacket was open, and under the jacket she was wearing her singed dress.

They all stood there staring at her, waiting to see what would happen next. Lena was in no hurry. "Why aren't you dancing?" she asked. "Come on, hop to it!" And she started to dance, imitating Shmakova's movements, spinning, twisting, until the music stopped. Silence descended upon the room.

"Too bad you didn't join in." Lena looked at each one in turn, slowly and deliberately, without flinching. "You're all so beautiful!" She walked around the room, looking at them, as if she hadn't seen them in a long time. "Just beautiful!"

Lena stopped suddenly in the middle of the room and tore the cap from her head. Everyone gasped at the sight of her shorn head. "But I'm a scarecrow! A scare-crow!" Lena patted her head. "A nice little cabbage-head with a big mouth. Right, Shmakova?" Lena smiled at Shmakova, stretching her lips as far as they would go. Then slowly and deliberately she turned her head so they could all see how ugly she was.

They stood staring at her, not knowing what to do.

Slowly and deliberately Lena walked toward

Dimka. "So sorry! I forgot to wish you a happy birthday," she said. "How silly of me. That's what I came here for, and I forgot."

Dimka stood there like a trapped animal, trying hard to avoid her eyes.

"Why are you ignoring me, Somov?" Lena slapped his shoulder. "Why are you trembling, you poor little thing! Could you be suffering because I'm a traitor? Eh? It must be rough on you. You're such a straight arrow, so brave and honest, and your friend is such a nasty girl who shouldn't be allowed to be anyone's friend. A tattletale! Snitch! Bitch!" She came over to Red. "Isn't that what you called me, Red?"

"I don't take it back," Red said.

"The time will come when you will, Tolya."

Red didn't respond. Lena hadn't expected him to; she had already moved on to Mironova. She looked into her eyes. "Hello, Iron Button!" she said.

"What now?" Mironova asked.

"I'm really surprised at you," Lena said with a sigh. "That's what."

"What are you surprised about?"

"That you, who are so righteous and just, would hang out with someone like Val. He's a skinner. Tsk, tsk, tsk. Do you know, he sells dogs at a ruble apiece to be skinned alive? You're a real fighter for truth and justice!"

"Watch it, you!" Val said.

"You are lying about Val," Shaggy said menacingly.

"Why, have you stopped skinning dogs, Val?" Lena pulled at Val's sleeve and then turned to Shaggy. "Why don't you hit me to shut me up! Come on, have you forgotten that strength is the most important thing in the world?"

"He will! He will hit you!" Val shouted. "Lying about me—I'll teach you!" He raised his fist.

"Oooh, I'm so afraid!" Lena laughed mockingly.

Val didn't dare hit her.

"Well, I'm getting bored with you all." Lena waved to everyone. "You got what you wanted. You win. I'm leaving tomorrow. You can be happy now. Let's hear it, all together now, one, two, three, 'Scarecrow is leaving! Scare-crow is leaving!' Well, come on! Cat got your tongues?"

Lena tore the flower off Shmakova's dress and pinned it to her jacket. She buttoned the jacket slowly, pulled the cap down over her head, and looked at them. "I pity you. I really do. You're pathetic, truly pathetic." Then she turned and left.

An eerie, incredible silence filled the room.

Suddenly Shaggy grabbed Val's arm. "What did Bessoltseva say about you?"

"She made it up!" Val shouted, pulling away.

"Then what's this?" Shaggy pulled the collar and leash from Val's pocket. "What's this?" He shook the leash in front of Val's terrified face.

"That?" Val was backing away from Shaggy. "That?"

"The tool of a skinner, that's what that is!" Red shouted.

Shaggy lunged at Val, who sidestepped and ran around the table, throwing chairs under Shaggy's feet, trying to keep out of his reach. "I'll tell Pete!" Val shouted. "He has friends! They'll show you! You can ask your father! He'll tell you about them!"

"Oh, my God." Red realized something. "Shaggy, did you hear that? Remember when your father was shot in the arm saving that elk from poachers? It was Pete and his friends!"

"So that was *you*!" Shaggy howled, launching himself at Val.

Val ran for the door, but Red tripped him. He fell; Shaggy fell on top of him.

Val managed to scramble up from under Shaggy, only to find that he had a collar and leash around his neck. The same leash he used to bring dogs to the skinner. The collar was tight around his neck and the leash was in Shaggy's hand.

"What are you doing?" Val cried in desperation. "You can't put a human on a leash!"

"Let's go outside," Shaggy said, pulling at the leash.

Going outside with Shaggy was what Val feared most. He tried to resist, tugging on the leash, digging in his heels. "Help me, please!" he begged. "Someone, help!"

No one moved.

"Shaggy!" he begged. "I won't do it again! Ever! I promise! It's all Pete's idea, ask Somov! He knows, he'll tell you, Pete's an animal!"

"Outside, I said." Shaggy pulled on the leash.

"Mironova, why don't you say something! Help me. I won't do it anymore!"

"Let him go," Mironova said.

Shaggy waited a second, then tossed the leash in Val's face.

"Get out!" Iron Button ordered Val. "You don't belong in our group."

"Why not? I'm one of the gang. One of you! Didn't I chase Scarecrow?"

"One of us?" Iron Button moved in on Val. "You, a skinner, one of us? Get out!"

Val put the leash in his pocket, grinned, and slunk out of the room.

Everyone was silent. Shaggy stood in the middle of the room with his head down and fists clenched.

"I didn't expect that from Scarecrow," Iron

127

Button said at last. "She let us have it. Not every-one could do that. Too bad she's a traitor, or I'd become her friend. You're all mush. Worth-less! You don't even know what you want. That's the end of our group. You make me sick. I'm leaving."

"What about the cake?" Dimka asked ner-vously. "We haven't had the cake yet."

"Cake? Now?"

"Why not?" Dimka said.

"Eat it yourself. I'm nauseated enough with-out it."

Mironova left, looking at no one.

"Mironova, wait!" Shaggy called after her. "I'll go with you!"

"Weren't you going to spend the night at my place?" Red asked.

"I changed my mind," Shaggy said. "I'm going home."

"Then I'll go with you," Red said, hurrying after Shaggy.

The door slammed behind them. Only the birthday boy, Shmakova, and Popov were left in the room.

"Maybe it was a mistake not to tell anyone?" Popov asked Shmakova softly. "Huh?"

"What are you talking about?" Dimka asked warily.

Shmakova smiled. She sensed the hour of her

triumph was near. "Popov and I," she sang happily, "you know, Dimka, Popov and I were . . ." She narrowed her eyes at Dimka—she liked watching him squirm. "Popov and I . . . that time . . ." She laughed and paused significantly, murmuring to herself.

"What about you and Popov?" Dimka asked.

Shmakova was in no hurry to answer. She wanted to torment him first, to get back at him for everything. Her mood was great and her plan was a total success. Dimka was destroyed, and therefore conquered and vanquished and hers once again. She was going to twist him around her little finger, make him her faithful slave forever. She was getting tired of Popov—he was a real drag.

"What about you and Popov?" Dimka asked again.

"Us?" Shmakova glowed. She did not take her eyes off Dimka's face. "We were under a desk."

Dimka smiled stupidly and asked, "When?"

"When you were having that nice chat with Margarita Ivanovna," Shmakova sang at last.

Dimka felt feverish. "You were . . . Margarita Ivanovna . . . ?"

"Under the desk. Us! Me and Popov!" Shmakova sang sweetly.

A sharp pang of fear made Dimka's heart thump like that of a mouse in the paws of a cat. What could he do? What? Beg for mercy? Or he could run away, move far, far away, never see any of them again. For a moment Dimka pictured himself walking down some dark alley in a strange city. It was cold, the autumn wind cutting through his jacket, rain lashing at his face. He had no friends, no one would invite him in to warm up and have a meal. He felt so sorry for himself.

"Why did you keep quiet?" Dimka babbled, his face contorted.

"We still have no intention of saying anything," Shmakova said. "Right, Popov?"

"You'll keep quiet?" Dimka smiled weakly, not understanding but hoping.

"But Shmakova, we have to tell," Popov said, not understanding what she meant.

Shmakova took a piece of cake from a plate and said, "Open wide!"

Popov obeyed.

Shmakova stuffed cake in his mouth and said, wiping crumbs from her fingers, "Be quiet and chew, or you'll choke. Everything got so complicated, it's hard to figure out what to do exactly. If we talk now, we won't be patted on the head for it. Understand, Popov? The three of us are tied together by the same rope. We have to stick close to each other." She went over to the stereo and put on a new record. "Let's dance and have a small party. It is your birthday, after all." She smiled at Dimka. "Give me a piece of cake."

Dimka handed her a piece.

Popov sighed noisily. "I've had it! I can't take any more. I'm leaving!"

"Where's he going?" Dimka was worried.

"Don't be scared. He won't snitch. He just needs some fresh air." Shmakova took a bite of the cake and said sweetly, "Delicious! Did your mother make it?"

Dimka sat down on the couch beside her.

Feeling very pleased with herself and her final victory over Dimka and Bessoltseva, Shmakova got up and danced while finishing her piece of cake, smiling mysteriously.

11

After a restless, sleepless night Nikolai Nikolaye-vich got up at dawn, washed in cold water, splashing it on his face to wake himself, and shaved carefully. Then he put on his suit and looked at himself in the mirror. *Yes, Lena was right. I should do something about my clothes.*

Grim and determined, he sat down at his desk and wrote for a long time. He put the paper in his pocket and walked into Lena's room. Her shaved head, so small and helpless-looking, lay quietly on the white pillow. She was fast asleep.

Nikolai Nikolayevich looked at his watch: It was eight. He decided not to wake Lena, she needed the rest. The boat wasn't leaving till eleven. Nikolai Nikolayevich started to hurry. He put on his coat and left the house, shutting the door quietly.

An hour later, the Bessoltsev house shuddered with loud hammering, as if a giant were striking it with a huge cudgel. The noise woke Lena. She sat up and looked out the window. She saw a hand placing a board across the window, and the room grew darker. Then the hammering started again.

Lena realized it was her grandfather boarding up the house.

She sprang out of bed and rushed outside in her nightgown. She did not feel the morning chill or the dewy wet grass on her bare feet. As if hypnotized, she stared at Nikolai Nikolayevich as he hammered nails into the old boards, covering all the windows. She looked up and saw that all four balconies were already sealed up. That made her particularly sad.

"Grandfather!" Lena called. "What are you doing?"

Nikolai Nikolayevich looked at the frightened, shaved Lena in her long white nightgown, barefoot, and he thought, *Just like Mashka!*

"More nails!" he shouted.

"You're boarding up the house?"

"I told you I need more nails!" he said. "And get dressed!"

Lena's teeth chattered as she dressed. Grandfather wasn't just taking her to her parents. He had decided to leave everything and go with her.

133

Leave his portraits!

His house!

His town!

Lena grabbed a bag of nails and brought it outside. Nikolai Nikolayevich took nails and boarded up the last two windows.

The Bessoltsev house was blind and deaf once more.

Nikolai Nikolayevich got down from the ladder.

Lena pressed her face into his chest and wept.

Now that the work was done, he sighed deeply. He was afraid he wouldn't have the strength to look at his boarded-up house.

"Come, child," said Nikolai Nikolayevich. "Why are we crying in public, like babies? Are we burying someone? On the contrary—we're doing something wonderful!"

After a quick breakfast, they turned off the electricity and gas, turned off the water main, and locked all the doors. They loaded two suitcases and a sack of apples on a wheelbarrow. Nikolai Nikolayevich put the painting of Mashka neatly wrapped in an embroidered towel, on top. They headed for the wharf, spurred on by an inner sadness they tried to hide from each other.

"Grandfather," Lena said, helping Nikolai Nikolayevich push the wheelbarrow, "I'm glad you're bringing *Mashka* with us." She picked up the portrait. "I'll carry it. We'll hang it in the best spot. And we won't be lonely. We'll look at *Mashka* and remember all the other portraits." She looked into his eyes. "Right, Grandfather?"

"Right, Lena!" said Nikolai Nikolayevich, and smiled.

"Why are you smiling? What are you happy about?"

"I have many reasons," Nikolai Nikolayevich said. "When we board the boat, I'll tell you everything in detail."

Suddenly they heard familiar cries: "Hurry! Get 'im!"

They heard whistling and running footsteps.

Lena ducked her head out of habit.

Nikolai Nikolayevich noticed and said, "Don't be frightened. Together we can face anyone. Do you hear? Anyone."

Lena nodded, listening to the approaching shouts.

"Yes, Grandfather," she replied, shivering a little.

Suddenly she turned to Nikolai Nikolayevich and handed him Mashka's portrait. "Hold this, please!" she said. And slowly, her head up high, she walked toward the approaching cries.

But what she saw was something she wasn't

prepared for: She saw Dimka—running! And after him, Mironova and Shaggy—almost their entire class—they were chasing Dimka! And she had been scared—what a joke!

Dimka ran clumsily, jogging along like a chicken with an injured wing, staying close to the fence to be less visible and constantly looking back, his face white with fear.

His pursuers' eyes burned with wrathful fire; their cheeks blazed with the color of the hunted and the hunters.

Someone grabbed Dimka's arm, someone else tripped him. He fell, jumped right up, squirmed out of their grasp, and ran on.

They ran past Nikolai Nikolayevich and Lena without noticing them, shouting, "Hold him!"

"Chase him toward the school!"

"We'll get you, you viper!"

They disappeared as quickly as they had appeared.

"Grandfather," Lena said softly, "does this mean Dimka confessed at last?"

"I guess it does," Nikolai Nikolayevich replied.

"What will happen now?" Lena asked, staring at Nikolai Nikolayevich.

"What will happen? They'll make a hero out of you now."

"Really?" Lena laughed. "What should I do?"

"Well, you can enjoy your victory. You can gloat."

"I'll run down to the school and see," Lena said.

"Don't, Lena," Nikolai Nikolayevich pleaded. "You don't kick a person when he's down."

"But I'm gloating!" Lena shouted. "I'm enjoying my victory!"

"Lena, wait!"

But Lena ran to join the hunters.

Nikolai Nikolayevich pushed the wheelbarrow and it turned over: The suitcases, the sack of apples, and Mashka's portrait all fell. Quickly Nikolai Nikolayevich righted the wheelbarrow, put the things back inside, and propped it by the fence. He took Mashka's portrait and hurried after Lena.

When Lena ran into the classroom, she saw Dimka standing on the windowsill. On his face was sheer terror.

"Get him!" shouted Val, grabbing Dimka's leg, trying to pull him down.

"Leave him alone." Iron Button stopped him scornfully. "Don't stick your filthy hands on him!"

Shaggy struck Val, and he moved away.

The gang moved toward Dimka, slowly, the way they had once moved in on Lena.

"Leave me alone!" he shouted. "Or I'll . . ."

He looked around. "Or I'll jump out the window!"

"No you won't," Mironova said. "You'd break a leg, and that hurts."

Dimka looked at Iron Button and started to open the window. . . .

Everyone took a step back.

"Get down," Lena said quietly.

Dimka saw Lena and jumped down.

"Our beautiful maiden is here!" Shmakova sang, but there was annoyance in her voice.

They surrounded Lena in a friendly crowd.

"Hi, Scarecrow!"

"Greetings!"

"So it turns out you're okay, Bessoltseva!" Shaggy slapped her back.

"Let me shake your hand," Red said, clowning as always.

"I'm glad you decided to stay." Iron Button came over, smiling. "Why didn't you tell us it was Somov? I guess you must have your reasons."

Realizing that they had forgotten about him, Dimka crept toward the door. He was turning the handle softly, hoping to slip away unnoticed. He wanted to get away while the attention was on Lena.

Suddenly he heard Mironova's voice. "Look at him! He's trying to sneak out!"

"Not a pretty picture," said Vasiliev.

Lena walked slowly toward Dimka. Iron Button walked next to her. "You trusted him," she said to Lena, "but now you can see his true face."

Lena came right up to Dimka. If she reached out, she could touch his shoulder.

"Slap him in the face!" Shaggy shouted.

Dimka turned his back on Lena.

"What did I tell you!" Iron Button's voice was triumphant. "The hour of retribution always comes! Justice triumphs! Hey, gang, we boycott Somov now!"

Everyone picked up the cry: "Boycott Somov! Boycott Somov!"

There, thought Lena. *Dimka has gotten what was coming to him.*

They surrounded Dimka and pulled him away from the wall.

"How about you?" Iron Button asked Lena. "Are you for the boycott?"

"No!" Lena said simply, and smiled her old, guilty smile.

"You've forgiven him?" Vasiliev was stunned.

"You fool," Shmakova said. "He set you up."

"What's wrong with you?" Iron Button wanted to know. "I don't understand you."

"I know what it's like to be chased like a hare. And I'll never do that to anyone, not even

139

Dimka. I'll die first!"

"How brave!" Shmakova snapped nastily. "You always have to be different."

"In that case, let's boycott the scarecrow too!" Val shouted. "Yeah!"

But no one paid any attention to him.

Just then, Margarita Ivanovna entered the classroom. "What's this? Didn't you hear the bell?" she said. "Quick, take your seats. I have some great news." Then Margarita Ivanovna saw Lena's head. "What happened to your hair?"

"She scorched her hair at the bonfire," Red said, "so she cut it."

"Bonfire?" asked Margarita Ivanovna. "What bonfire?"

But the great news Margarita Ivanovna wanted to share with them made her forget Lena's hair. "Children, children! Attention!" She rapped her knuckles on the desk. "Listen!" Margarita Ivanovna's voice was very happy. "Lena Bessoltseva will tell us the great news."

"What news?" Lena didn't know what she was talking about.

"Didn't your grandfather tell you?" Margarita Ivanovna was surprised. "Then I will. Children, Nikolai Nikolayevich Bessoltsev, Lena's grandfather, has given his house and his collection of paintings to our town. The paintings have belonged to the Bessoltsev family for many generations. They are the work of their ancestor, an artist who lived in the nineteenth century! Now Nikolai Nikolayevich is donating them. We will have a museum in our town!"

"A museum?" Lena couldn't believe her ears.

"How much did he get?" Val asked.

"I just told you, he donated everything!"

"He gave it away? For free?"

"Of course," Margarita Ivanovna replied. "Do you realize what a generous gesture that is?"

Val was confused. Having a lot of money, he thought, was what was most important. And here was someone who was giving away his riches. His house, which was worth thousands. And his paintings, which were probably worth millions.

The whole class was impressed. They stared at Lena, the expressions on their faces ranging from delight to confusion and embarrassment.

It was so quiet, so infinitely quiet, that the hesitant knock at the door felt like a loud bang. The door opened a crack and Nikolai Nikolaye-vich appeared holding *Mashka* in his hands.

"Excuse me," he said. "I'm sorry I must interrupt. Lena, we'll be late for the boat."

"Nikolai Nikolayevich!" Margarita Ivanovna pulled him into the room. "Please, come inside."

"We have to leave; we'll be late," Nikolai Niko-layevich said. "I'm sorry to interrupt."

"Allow me to express our gratitude," Margarita Ivanovna said. "You are so wonderful! So wonderful! I've never met anyone like you. Thank you! I swear, I'm going to burst into tears. . . ."

"Excuse me." Nikolai Nikolayevich was happy and sad at the same time: He had wanted to tell Lena himself.

"Grandfather, did you do that because of me?" Lena asked. "*All* the family portraits? How will you live without them?"

"I have you, child. You are the most important thing to me." Nikolai Nikolayevich, feeling more and more embarrassed, smiled at the young faces before him as if trying to look into their souls, and raised Mashka's portrait over his head. "This painting is very dear to me. It is of Mashka, my great-aunt. She was a teacher." Then he added softly, "I'm giving this painting to your school."

"Grandfather!" Lena exclaimed. "Grandfather, not *Mashka*!"

"It's time for us to leave," Nikolai Nikolayevich said, taking Lena's hand. "The boat won't wait for us."

"Let me go with you," Margarita Ivanovna said.

"No, no," Nikolai Nikolayevich said. "That's not necessary."

"Then let me accompany you to the principal's office. He wants to thank you personally," said Margarita Ivanovna.

For the last time Lena's shaved head moved through the door, for the last time Nikolai Nikolayevich's big patches flashed before them, and they disappeared, leaving behind a guilty silence.

Vasiliev sighed. "Oh, damn!" he said in disgust.

"And all because of Somov!" Shaggy rushed over to Dimka with his fists clenched. "You scum!"

"Boycott Somov!" shouted Iron Button. "Let's vote!"

But they didn't have time, because Margarita Ivanovna was back in the room. "I'll be right back. Just wait here quietly. And what's this about a boycott? Again? Who this time? And why?"

"Somov! That's who!" Iron Button was pale with indignation. "He's a double traitor!"

"Somov a traitor. . . . I don't understand."

"Didn't he tell you that we cut class to go to the movies?" Mironova asked.

"Yes, he did," said Margarita Ivanovna, not understanding what Mironova was getting at.

"And we thought it was Bessoltseva!" cried Mironova.

"We chased her and beat her up," Vasiliev said. "We taunted her. And Somov didn't own up."

"And you didn't do anything, Margarita Ivanovna," Mironova said accusingly.

"Do anything?" Margarita Ivanovna repeated, looking at Mironova. "I thought Somov had told you." She looked at Dimka. "How could you, Somov?"

Dimka was silent.

"Bessoltseva took the blame," Mironova explained. "She wanted to help Somov, and he betrayed her."

"That's why she was waiting for me that day!" Margarita Ivanovna suddenly understood that she had let Lena down. She was so upset by the realization that she paid no attention to the kids shouting about Dimka Somov.

"So, who's for the boycott?" Mironova raised her hand again.

"I for one am against it," Red said unexpectedly. "I despise Somov. But I'm not going to boycott him. If Lena was against it, so am I. I always go along. Because I'm Red and I don't want to be different." He was almost crying now, his voice unsteady. "But I've had it! You can shout and call me 'Red' all day long, I'll still do things my own way, the way I think is right." And he breathed a sigh of relief.

Margarita Ivanovna looked at her watch: The boat was due to leave in ten minutes.

She turned to Dimka. "How could you do such a thing?" In her anger she grabbed him by the shoulders and shook him. "Answer me!"

"You think I was the only one who kept quiet?" Dimka yelled. "Shmakova and Popov knew all about it too!"

"What?" cried Mironova.

"We were under a desk together," Popov said.

"And you kept your mouth shut?" Mironova glared at Popov.

"Because of me," Shmakova sang out.

"While another person suffered," Red said.

"I was waiting for Dimka to confess," Shmakova said. "He kept weaseling out of it." She turned to Dimka. "By the way, Dimka, Popov and I didn't snitch on anyone."

Shaggy shook his fist at Shmakova.

Popov rushed over and grabbed his hand. "Take it easy! Shmakova is so wonderful and generous."

"Wonderful? Generous?" Shaggy cried out. "Take a good look at her, you jerk."

"So I'm not wonderful and generous," Shmakova said meanly. "Those kinds of people get used."

"She's just saying that," Popov said.

"I don't need you to defend me," Shmakova

said. "And I don't want to sit with you anymore. I like to change places," she said in her singsong voice: "I'll sit with poor old Dimka, because everyone has abandoned him." She took Lena's seat.

Popov stood there not knowing what to do with himself.

Shaggy looked at his fist. "I thought strength and order were the most important things in the world. I thought I'd live in the forest, like my father, and all the Vals and all the Petes would be afraid of me." He pushed the fist in his face. "I'd like to punch myself. . . ."

"Hey, everybody!" Popov suddenly shouted. "Shmakova is sitting with Somov, and he's a traitor!"

"Right," Mironova said. "Let's boycott the traitor." She raised her hand. "Who's for it?"

Only Popov raised his hand.

"You creeps!" Iron Button looked at the class with scorn. "Then I'll boycott Somov myself. No one ever escapes retribution! It catches up with everyone sooner or later, like Somov!" Her voice broke, and she began to sob.

"Iron Button is crying," Shmakova sang. "There must be an earthquake somewhere."

"You're all just like my mother. She thinks only of herself. She believes you can get away with anything as long as it's covered up! And

you're just like her! All of you! Just like her!"
Iron Button wept bitterly.

"Everyone wants what's best for themselves,"
said Val. "That's a fact of life."

"What about the Bessoltsevs?" Vasiliev asked.

"The Bessoltsevs!" Val sneered. "They're
weird and we're normal!"

"You're normal? Or me? Why don't you say
that Somov is normal too? We're animals," Red
said grimly. "That's what we are, animals. We
should be kept in cages in the zoo."

Margarita Ivanovna listened in silence. The
more she listened, the worse she felt. How could
she have been so insensitive to their needs?

She went over to Mironova and put her hand
on her shuddering shoulder.

Mironova tossed off her hand. "I don't need
your pity," she said. "Leave me alone. Where
were you when we needed you?"

I deserve that, thought Margarita Ivanovna.

The sound of the siren signaling the boat's
departure reached the class and vibrated
throughout the classroom. Margarita Ivanovna
went to the window. "The boat's leaving," she
said sadly.

Everyone rushed to the windows — except
Somov.

They stood by the windows hoping for one
last glimpse of the boat that was taking away

147

Lena. The scarecrow who had changed their lives.

Red moved from the windows and looked at the painting Nikolai Nikolayevich had left. His face changed. "It's her!" he shouted.

They all turned and looked at Mashka's portrait.

"It's Lena!" Iron Button cried out.

"It's Scarecrow," Shaggy whispered.

"Wrong!" Vasiliev said. "It's Bessoltseva."

They stared at *Mashka*: Her shaven head on the long thin neck looked like an early spring flower — innocent, radiant.

Red went to the blackboard and scrawled in big letters:

SCARECROW, FORGIVE US!